Barred

Short Stories

Derek O'Gorman

An Imprint of Sulis International Press
Los Angeles | Dallas | London

BARRED: SHORT STORIES

Cover design by Megan Rose for Sulis International Press. Cover photo by Photo by Yves Alarie.

ISBN (print): 978-1-958139-22-6
ISBN (eBook): 978-1-958139-23-3

Published by Riversong Books
An Imprint of Sulis International
Los Angeles | Dallas | London

www.sulisinternational.com

Contents

Barred

00.45am

He could still make Lennox's. Lennox's stayed open till one.

There are no bouncers there like, not in Lennox's.

And he could mangle a bag of chips. He could bunk the gate at The College, darker now, not like earlier, nothing stirring, across the Quad: "you shouldn't do it until you graduate", they said: t'would jinx you", they said.

They shouldn't have worried. It wasn't for me, Law or Arts, neither of them, and the father will never let me forget it.

"Thousands wasted…thousands."

Out at the back of The Boole…

Shur, that fiend didn't even go to school and a library named after him.

…and onto College Road. Not a peep, not till Monday.

The neighbours, a begrudging clannish shower delighted I couldn't hack it, the college dropout. Never said it outright, but I could see it in their

faces, "Your father will look after you. Born with a silver spoon in your mouth, you were Murphy boy."

Lennox's quiet.

"Battered sausage?"

Battered.

"And the drink?"

Battered.

"Do you want a drink or don't you?"

"Make that two chips will ya. I'm feeling lucky."

"Take your change there now and sling your hook."

Isn't that women in a nutshell for you though. Tarting themselves all up and as soon as you make a move.

8.15am

"Just watch where you're putting your hands Sean, will ya! I'm late enough for work as it is already."

"Why don't you just skip work for one day, Sandra girl."

"We can't afford it. Now let me go. You're hurting me. And what are you going to do all day?"

"I said I'm going to find a job for myself, didn't I?"

"When though?"

"Today alright!"

"Good. Now let me go, I said. I mean it!"

Bitch.

He didn't mean the slap. She drew him out.

00.45am

Sling your hook. Who does she think she is talking to?

"Bitch."

She drew me out. I'd never hurt a fly. I love her.

"Did you say something there boy, did you?"

"Me? no girl, didn't say a word."

"Good, so take your food and go."

"The day I'm after having, trouble is the last thing I'm looking for."

You can't talk to a girl anymore now. You'd get the shit kicked out of yourself in two minutes you would. Cork isn't what it used to be at all, Patrick's Street, you'd be bricking yourself walking through it.

8.15am

He could make the site by half eight. That would show Sandra he meant business. He could cut down through Wellington Road and there in front of him he could take his pick: sites all over Cork. Work for everyone: Turks, Syrians, Poles.

Something for everyone, and all I want is a start.

"I'd have something on Monday if you want."

"Monday."

"Show your face for half seven with your safe-pass, and we will get you started."

Yes! Didn't I tell her.

He could call round to the father now, show his face, tell him his news, a job, got it himself, no favours needed. He could be there in twenty minutes, put the pride in his back pocket and tap him for a few pounds. He would have it back to him next week.

Get Sandra something nice, make it up to her, good and proper. End to a perfect day.

9.00am

"Got a job for myself."

"Don't I have plenty of work for you if you want it?"

"My own job Dad."

"And is that why you came all the way down here: just to tell me you got your own job."

"And I need a favour. Just till next week like."

"A favour?"

"I'm in a small jam, that's all."

"Another one."

Please don't make me beg.

"Tis nothing. I just need some money to tide me over."

"Your mother and I are in Spain next week-flying tonight."

Jesus, I'll have it for them when they get back. Tis money in the bank. Their own son.

"We don't have sight or sound of you for six months, and you turn up here out of the blue looking for a bail out!"

"Ye threw me out."

Didn't even give me a chance.

"We asked you to leave Sean. There's a difference, we couldn't put up with you anymore."

Couldn't put up with me.

"None of us could."

I should have phoned her.

"And how is mam?

"She worries. She needs the break."

"And Kate?"

"Your sister is fine boy, busy with exams, but what would you know about that?"

Jesus, I haven't got time for this today. The third degree, not again: "Am I still drinking? smoking myself stupid? We want you to get help. There's plenty of people you can call on to start again, professional people." I need money, that's what I need!

"I just can't do it, Sean."

"I just can't do it", but he can go to Spain and ask me to leave the house. Tell me I'm not welcome in my own home. Ten o'clock in the morning, and I'm screwed. I need to phone Sandra and explain. I didn't mean it. She drew me out.

10.00am

"Jesus Sean, what do you want? I told you not to be phoning me at work."

"We need to talk Sandra girl."

"After lunch, so outside *Electric*, quarter to two."

He would try the site once more. Show them he was keen.

"Like I said earlier, there will be plenty of work for you, Monday, if you want it."

Of course, I want it, and he is still banging on about the safe pass. Jesus, I'm only asking for a start like, something to get me going.

"Look. I explained it twice, what you need to do. I told you this morning, and I'm telling you again now. Get your paperwork in order and we will have a chat then."

Paperwork! A Corkman.

"And what about all those refugee fiends, did you go looking for their paperwork!"

"Right, I've had enough of your shite. Out!! If I see you round here again, I'll get the guards for you!"

More shit, taking the stuff, all day, I am, wrecking my head now. The old doll first thing this morning, and then the old man has a cut. I'll have to square things with Sandra.

1.45pm

"Keep your voice down, Sean. You're making a scene."

"We need to talk Sandra."

"No."

"Christ girl, will you give me a chance to explain myself?"

"No…it's over alright. I don't want to see you. I don't want you around, and I don't want to listen to any more of your bullshit."

He shouldn't have taken the 50, but he asked, and she agreed.

Needs must.

"Sound Sandra girl. I'll pay you back."

"Don't bother, and I don't want to see you round when I get home."

He headed to *Soho* for one, just the one to settle himself, and get his head around the day. The place was dead, half two, and he had the whole gaff to himself. So, he had a second one. Plasma screens and flashing images of Roy Keane and some Eastern European fiend flattened on the grass behind him. Roy striding on with that arrogant smirk of his.

Walked out on his country, that fella.

"Look, we don't want any trouble. Just finish your drink and move on."

"Left his country down!"

"Right enough that's it -out you go-you're barred! Do you hear me? Barred!"

The Grand Parade shifted all around him now, nobody looking, but everyone giving him the wide berth. A young mother grabbed her child's hand.

Only a child herself.

"He left his country down!"

"You are making a bit of a racket there boy."

"Sorry Guard, sorry about that."

"Good. Move along there so, will you like a good man."

Sound.

The number 14 from *The Imperial* brings him out to this dealer fiend he knows at Dennehy's Cross, passing the College Main Gates, busy, and the coaches lined up at The Gateway to bring home the weekenders.

They told me nearly 20% dropped out and not to beat myself up over it, and that I could defer, try again. Same spiel I got from mam, and they wanted to know how I was feeling, told me not to bottle it up, to talk. It would make me feel better. The father was having none of it.

"If it was left to me, I'd have a big red flag beside your name and barred out of the place for life!"

A girl gets on, iPhone, and flashes a pink g string as she goes to sit. The whole bus, hoping she'll bend again for her bag or something, but not him. He's off at Tesco Express, and it's another bag he is after.

4.30pm

"What are you doing here?"

"I need something to take the edge off."

"Didn't I tell you before not to be calling here looking for yokes!"

"Look, are you going to give me the stuff or not?"

"Twenty euros so."

"Twenty!"

"You owe me thirty already."

"Go on then, take the scabby twenty."

"And you are not taking the stuff here. I'm not minding you for the day."

So, he pops them down at the back of the church.

Daycint! and the Virgin Mary doing the *Riverdance* on the altar.

"Go on Mary girl you mad thing."

"I'm afraid you are going to have to leave."

"What do you mean I can't put my feet up! Mary! Mary!! Mary!!!"

Bounced out of The Descent of the Holy Ghost.

I will have to watch the rest of it in The Honan.

"Two St. Patrick's?"

"Yes mam. We are doing it in History."

"Is that what we are sending you to college for, two St. Patrick's? Hah! You'd be better off going into the Church and saying a prayer for yourself."

"And I'll light a candle for you mam!"

"Do that boy. Two St. Patrick's…."

And I was true to my word. Had the whole place to myself, time to take it all in. The Honan in all its glory, but not today, today Judas Iscariot has me in the horrors.

Exit stage left.

7.00pm

He could be at the house in ten minutes, just a quick call for a cup of tea. He wouldn't tell anyone if Kate didn't. A cup of tea and a few *bob* for a bite to eat.

"They don't want you in the house Sean, not after the last night."

"Forget that Kate will ya. I was steamed to the gills that night."

"One cup of tea, and then you're gone, right? I'm up the walls, seriously."

My own sister turned against me. A cup of tea plain and simple like, no bother. Wants me to beg on my hands and knees.

"Taking shit all day, I am, and now this. Just don't be annoying me, Kate!"

She never saw the hit coming, didn't stand a chance.

She was going to throw me out, my own sister, with nothing to my name and my hands hanging. Don't make me laugh.

He knew all the old hiding places50...100...150...200 euro.

Imagine the father's face if he saw me now with a couple of hundred to tide me over. The money he couldn't spare for his own son.

10.00pm

He grabbed a taxi at The Lough and passed through Kinsale roundabout climbing; lights of the city in the distance, onwards and upwards the whole city spread out beneath him; tiny dots, Sandra, the foreman, the father, his dealer, tiny dots and Kate with her mangy cup of tea. The parents getting away from it all.

Told him I was in a jam, and he wouldn't listen. Won't expect me to see them off. He'll listen now. Won't expect me at the airport.

Dots everywhere as the queue in departures snakes all around him.

Claustrophobic.

Dots and he is disconnected, overheating. Pictures no sound, dots, London, Paris, Prague, Majorca for the sun, and there he is…the father.

Doing his stuff at the desk with me mam, looking tired, looking like she needs a break and like I'm the last person she needs to meet.

And he watches the pair of them trundling to the escalator, him leading the way and her a pace behind. Watching his parents; keeping his news to himself.

I couldn't do that to mam, not tonight.

11.30pm

And it's another taxi into town then.

20 euros! From the airport. Ryanair will fly me to Amsterdam for that. Another robber.

And a breeze blowing through Washington Street that would skin you. Head down, minding his own business.

You could get the shit kicked out of you for no reason.

He could still make Lennox's. Lennox's stayed open till one.

00.45am

"You heard her. Take it outside and let other people get served, you college pussy."

Some Polish fiend telling me what to do in my own city, a: "college pussy". The father would be proud of that. All that money well spent.

"Piss off back to your own country boy."

That's Cork for you nowadays, not safe anymore. Jumped, jumped outside Lennox's, some Polish fiend hops me for no reason like, langer, and skies the money too. Robbed me-every cent-200 euro, enough to tide me over. That's all I wanted. Gone, like Sandra, the parents, like Kate.

He would be home in an hour. He could spend the night now. Nothing to stop him now, a roof over his head, and Kate lying battered in the pool of blood where he left her.

Battered. Never changed her stash in all the years. Gone now though Kate. Jumped me.

"Do you want a chip, Kate? Brought you back some like I used to, for the all-nighters, remember those? Still mad for the books and the college eh Kate and the parents dead proud of you. Kate? I get short Kate, you know that. It just happens sometimes, like the time I broke your arm on the swing, messing. I snap. A cup of tea Kate girl in my own home, not too much to ask. I was going to tell them at the airport that we were at it again, like old times, horseplay, but I hadn't the heart. I will phone them in the morning and stay at home with you to-night girl. Where else would I be going after the day I've had? Barred from most places at this stage. Probably even barred from Lennox's."

The Station Master

His father had fished out of Kinsale. What he didn't know about the sea wasn't worth knowing and he shared every morsel of it with his son because the father knew, knew he was a natural.

"Made for it," he would reassure a sceptical mother.

And on June evenings, after their daily swim:

"The only time for one," he used to say, his father speaking to him in conspiratorial tones as he dried him off coarsely.

"When your time comes to be called, you must face that music alone."

The son had heard that a hundred times over, never understanding it, not as a ten-year-old child, but it had stayed with him and when his father's time did come, one dark October evening six years later, a premature cardiac event, he had used it on the altar as the chief mourner; friends and neighbours agreeing he had done his father proud for someone so young.

And he remembered him today as he made his way to the station house, remembered the receding hairline as he himself had now and especially his hands, bony, well-worn and the wedding ring that he wore on his little finger the only show of ostentatiousness. His mother's ring, a woman who hated the sea, boats and old fishermen and a woman he had never known who had gone out one morning to buy him a bicycle for Christmas and never came back. His father then, in his wisdom, bought him a chemistry set instead, and all he wanted to do was blow up the house. She did come back after, as it happened, to Ballinspittle, across the bridge, but a different world, and she lived out her days quite happily, by all accounts, with the local postman, while ten miles away his father lived in the hope of reuniting her with ring she had discarded on the draining board.

And so, he remembered all this as he approached the station house, with the distant shrills of day trippers and seagulls drifting across the harbour. He noticed his own hands as he worked the lock, familiarly stubborn, the wedding ring on his little finger now as the final jangle broke his train of thought. He stopped short. No longer seeing him, he walked quietly in and stood in silence.

The smell of the sea and the momentary murmur before the lights clicked into action, four clicks. Someone had forgotten to recoil the hose after washing out the rib. He made a mental note and quickly corrected himself. The citation in its pride of place on the station wall caught his eye. The crews' idea and not one he had encouraged, but they had convinced him; had said it could never be taken away from him, what he did that night, his legacy. Stopping, he read it once more:

"*For valour on both treacherous and heavy seas.*"

It was a source of comfort to him now, another reminder of what had been:

"*At no little risk to himself.*"

And he remembered that night when everyone wanted to shake his hand, Olivia as proud as punch, her husband John, a hero:

"*The West Cork Community Award Winner.*"

That rescue made him. A legacy for others now to strive towards going forward. A shift he hadn't even been on call for until it had all kicked off at home. That's how he remembered it. A twist of fate, the first night she hit him. Olivia screaming standing over him, a thing of nothing, but she had drawn blood. The woman he loved, married.

They were part of a gang from High Street who hung around together, and they married in 95. A natural progression, and "made for each other" was the consensus, but he had chosen to misread the tell-tale signs, dismissing them as a petulance he could somehow manage. So, he got a steady job above at the Community Hospital cleaning and embraced the newness of it all, the responsibilities, and for six months it was good until he found himself needing the long working hours to keep himself out of the house and the lifeboat to keep him out of her way. They sought advice from the priest (her friend's idea) who thought a child would help keep her occupied (his words), but nothing happened and there were no treatments afforded on a cleaner's wages. Nothing more was said and after that he threw himself into the station with a newfound zeal. She threw herself into the drink.

He never forgot his first recovery, a horrible day and a young lad, fishing with his dog, swept off the rocks. The parents clinging to hope on the beach as they set off.

"There's a cave, he could get shelter there," he explained, not believing a word of it, while they hung on every syllable.

When they arrived, it was the dog he saw first. A terrier soaked to the bone and shivering on the rocks, staring forlornly at the mouth of the cave. Even the dog knew. On the way back, nobody spoke. At home, he found her slumped in the shower when he needed someone to talk to, to hold. Instead, he forced himself to put her to bed with those same hands that had cradled a seventeen-year-old's body only an hour earlier. Alone again, he threw up with nothing to throw. It all went downhill after that.

Soon he was volunteering every hour God gave him, working his way up, John Cunningham, a leader of men escaping from one woman. The beatings became more frequent, but the station covered everything; hard physical work, covered the knocks, the cuts, the bruises, the truth and then gave him his day in the sun.

The call had come through at nine o'clock a release from his own distress, the perfect storm and by the time they had arrived, the yacht was already capsized and running aground; big eight-and ten-foot waves forcing it towards the cliff face while a figure frozen with fear clung on for life. He saw the wave before it hit, fifteen feet high and travelling almost in slow motion, straight and firm, a complete contrast to the turmoil around it, majestic, a ferocious power but also a thing of silence… 3…2…1…whoosh…throwing the casualty into the air like a rag doll and John willing a connection to happen, willing it with a desire he never felt in his life.

"You can do this! You can swim! Come on!! You can make this!!! Swim! Gotcha!! You beauty!!"

Engulfed in a dead man's grip and a final drag on board as one. He lay there, and it began, slowly rising out of control, manic, a laugh like never before piercing the night sky. Tears of joy, tears of pain, primal. Ten years of hurt:

"Bravery above and beyond the call of duty."

When he got home, she had gone to the pub anyway.

By June 2006, the rumours were at their peak, a different pub every night, a different one-night stand. Tourists mostly, passing through, and he did what he always did, turned a deaf ear…until one night:

"I don't want your acquaintances coming back to the house."

"I'll bring back whoever I want."

He moved out the following day, and he wondered what his father would have made of it all. The man who had waited stoically for his wife to come back from the shops, bicycle in tow. An Irish separation, keeping it in the family, one might say, him in a flat in town, and they'd meet out shopping in *Aldi* or even down the local. Another wedding ring discarded in a box at the back of his locker amongst the washers and the WD 40. Civility broke out.

For the crew he was still the go-to guy if someone was in trouble off the Old Head, and he commanded the respect he had never mastered within his own four walls, but alone thoughts began to consume him of how he had become, one-dimensional, defined, and it wasn't enough anymore. Often, he would now find himself distracted even at the most perilous moments, with lives in the balance, adrift, a slow realisation that what had kept him afloat all these years was slipping away, that deep down the edge was gone.

The first time they made contact, it was loose change; would he get a bag of Xanax out of the clinic and drop it to a dealer in Cork? Three hundred into the hand. They had seen a weakness, but the adrenaline was pumping, and it felt good. By the third run, the hospital was on to him, fired, no questions asked. Swept under the carpet for a pillar of the community, no one knowing, not the crew, not Olivia. A lucky break he hadn't deserved. A luck that left him to his own devices and wanting to feel that edge again. He was hooked.

At the height of that summer, he had it off to a T, collect the coke in Dublin, store it and deliver it to the dealers in Cork. Three hundred a trip. Hand to mouth stuff, but he wanted something more, enough to set himself up and sort out his responsibilities. Those commitments he had once embraced now a suffocating noose around his neck, still contributing to a roof over her head and no end in sight. The price of freedom. A weight that needed lifting once and for all.

And so, once a month, he took the risk, taking the rib out into the harbour to collect 150,000 worth of coke off the Old Head, deliver it and pocket 7k. John risking it all in a battle against the sea and the rocks, what he was born for-celebrated for.

When they raided the flat, he hadn't even the stuff planked. The price of complacency: a hundred and fifty grands worth of coke on the kitchen table, his ledger, names, addresses-the lot. There was no carpet big enough to sweep this under, cautioned and charged his free legal aid (a friend of the fathers) braced him for seven to ten years. At that first meeting, the advice he couldn't afford suggested that he might come to some arrangement with herself to walk into court together, a real show of support.

"It would look good."

Olivia, on hearing this, was agreeable to a fault, the woman who had beaten seven shades of shite out of him, but as the date loomed closer, he had reneged on his part of that deception. He couldn't put her through that.

The service had been more than decent, giving him this time alone to clear out his locker and hand back his keys. A dignity he felt he didn't deserve. He read the citation one last time, and he pictured his father again, reminding him of how the sea was like life itself, cruel and never to be trusted; a reminder of what he had become:

"The West Cork Community Award Winner."

He wouldn't take that, his legacy, thirty years of service. That was a memory he would leave for someone else to erase. His locker contained little of value to him. Odds and ends he had never got round to putting in the bin, and today was no different. He would go up those courthouse steps on his own tomorrow, face that music alone, like father, like son. He had done him proud once, but there was no solace in that, not this time. Those chips were cashed in. Slowly, he removed the tight-fitting wedding ring from his little finger and placed it also in a final resting place amongst the washers and discarded spray cans.

These memories of his father dimmed as John Cunningham made to leave the station house one last time, his last act as station master, and as he left, he remembered, just for a moment, a woman he had never known and a postman in Ballinspittle.

Opportunities

July 1967
The South East of Ireland
Sunday

Every Sunday after twelve mass Maura O'Neill called into Kelly's for *The Sunday Press*. Maura played *Spot the Ball* with a religious zeal, and she was totally convinced that one Sunday she would open the paper to the revelation that her X from the previous week's competition had brought home the bacon.

Maura had also been schooled by her mother, God rest her, to never leave the church at the close of mass with the priest still on the altar, but the new curate Fr O'Sullivan was obstinate in nature and stood transfixed as the choir laboured through to the bitter end of the hymn of their choice, and he never moved until the very last note. Her mother was above in the graveyard now, and Maura was slowly revising that unwritten courtesy. Now on Sundays, as the choir struggled through the first verse of the last hymn, she had taken to making her exit, leaving Fr O'Sullivan in his pious pose facing the tabernacle. She would then edge past the men chatting in hushed tones in the yard, mount her bicycle that had seen better days, and head for Kelly's.

Often, she would stop at the graveyard, pause, and say a quick prayer for her dear departed mother and then down the hill with the wind at her back and past the headland. From there she could see the sweep of the entire bay; on winter Sundays a bleak canvas; angry waves crashing against the cliff face and a blanket of greyness. Today she hadn't the time to admire this transformed vista; the sea an azure blanket; ripples few and far between, and already a couple of sail boats dotted in the bay. There was a haze of heat.

It will be packed today, she thought to herself as the bike picked up a head of steam on the descent to the beach.

Maura squeezed every ounce out of the bike on the final approach because today Maura had news and not just any old news, big news, and Maura knew that around these parts that news of this nature needed to be shared early and as quickly as possible for maximum effect. Then the final round of the bend before it came into view:

Kelly's Convenien e Store

sitting adjacent to the beach; the missing *c* a testament to the many losing battles the building had with sand and sea over a generation.

Nothing, a lick of paint wouldn't sort, Maura thought to herself as she dismounted quickly, leaving the bicycle balanced against the wall.

If ever a place needed a man. Briefly, she remembered Frank Kelly.

Where did those ten years go?

Maura approached the door knowing only too well that inside also had seen better days, knowing that on Sundays she would find John Power present in his own losing battle with the fruit machine. She opened the door, and it rattled shut behind her.

"Catherine," she called out as she moved quickly across to the counter.

"Catherine! Is she in John?", she enquired in exasperation, but John Power never broke concentration and stayed engrossed in this latest bout of man versus machine.

"Catherine!!" Maura called out again, making her way to the counter where she began ringing the counter bell incessantly, drowning out the fanfare of the fruit machine. This time John Power did raise a look.

"Hey," he answered in annoyance, shooting her a scowling glance.

"Catherine, they'll be in on top of us in two minutes. Jesus Mary and Joseph!" Maura continued before turning her fire on John.

"And come away from that bloody thing you," she chided as she caught her own reflection in the *Jacobs Biscuits* mirror that hung behind the counter. She fixed herself quickly.

"How do I look?" she asked, this time to no one in particular.

"Just look at the state of me!"

This time Catherine Kelly did emerge, a diminutive woman in her mid-fifties with mousy hair. She hadn't slept well, and this lack of sleep was etched in her face. Her green eyes that once sparkled were this morning dimmed. Her son Robert was home for the first time since her husband Frank had passed, but there had been little talk of note between them in the first twenty-four hours. She could barely contain her annoyance at the incessant ringing.

"For the love of God Maura what in heaven's name has got into you!"

Maura O'Neill was still in full flight, barely drawing breath.

"They were above at twelve mass in the village Catherine. They could be down any second now. Jackie Kennedy and the kids."

"And?" Catherine replied nonplussed.

"Won't she be wanting the Sunday papers and some sweets for the children."

Catherine moved along the counter and subtly withdrew the offending bell to the cereal shelf.

"I won't be serving her any papers," she replied softly.

Maura O'Neill took a step back from the counter, aghast.

"You'll be telling me next that she's only arrived a day at The Manor, and you have her barred already."

"Not a bad idea," John Power interjected sarcastically, enjoying this exchange between the two women from his vantage point.

"Not barred," Catherine continued offhandedly, "but didn't I tell you last Sunday that I was stopping the Sunday papers over that snake Dan Daly selling them out of the boot of his car above at the church. Doesn't want anyone to earn a brass farthing, that fella."

The news seemed to catch Maura O'Neill off-guard and momentarily she was lost for words.

"Do you remember that conversation, Maura, how I explained that to you?"

Maura gathered herself: "Shur, I took no notice of that. I just put that down to you being your cantankerous self."

Catherine ignored this retort: "And how I explained that after almost twenty years you would have to be going somewhere else for your *Sunday Press*."

Outside, a car pulled up and Maura cut her off quickly as she crossed to the window.

"Listen...Is that a car?"

As Maura strained to look out over the frosted glass, John finally stepped away from the fruit machine.

"I'll tell you what you could do Catherine, hang a big Russian flag out your window there. That would drum up a bit of business for you right enough, bring the boys down from R.T.E and all."

"In Russia they'd have your likes breaking stones in Siberia," Maura shot back sharply before Catherine could answer.

"And what did the Yanks ever do for you?" John answered, rising to the bait.

"Ah, your brain is scrambled from standing in front of that thing all day long," Maura replied, waving her arms dismissively. She moved away from the window, shrugging in disappointment.

"Just a few day trippers arriving early. She must have gone straight back to The Manor after mass."

"Probably bought *The Sunday Press* from Dan Daly," John Power quipped, determined to get the last word in.

"Hand us out some change there, Catherine girl."

Catherine carefully counted out the coins for John and he returned to play on the fruit machine. There was a brief silence and the music from the machine filled the void.

"I'll see you out, Maura," Catherine offered, and the women went to stand outside. A light breeze cooled them there and the sounds of the day trippers echoed around them. Catherine couldn't help wondering how the day would pan out. She'd probably sell a few ice creams, and some sweets later, but not enough to keep the wolf from the door. She thought of her son Robert. He had hardly spoken last night, and now it was well past midday, and he was still in bed. She was glad to have him home, but the initial euphoria was short-lived, and she was now wondering what it was all about.

"You didn't think of going up to the church yourself? Maura asked.

"I did not," Catherine answered, throwing her a look, but Maura was finding her voice again.

"I never saw a crowd like it. I thought you might have made an exception the day that was in it. The little fella is only handsome, the spit of his father, God rest him."

"I'll not darken their door again, Maura, not after what they put me through," Catherine said pointedly.

"Fr Flanagan was only following the bishop's instructions that time. The Church has very specific laws in relation to suicide, you know."

Catherine stiffened. "And that gave them the right to deny my Frank a proper burial in the family plot."

Maura knew better to go down that familiar road, so she mounted her bicycle and made off with a jaunty wave. Catherine watched her go; dress flapping in the wind, and again she thought of her husband Frank. The verdict had been death by misadventure, drowning at sea. Maura and she had clashed many times over the years on the church's stance and watching her leave she allowed herself a smile at the thought of Maura leaving empty-handed without her *Sunday Press* and now peddling like the clappers back to the churchyard to get her paper from Dan Daly.

I'm a right bitch, she thought to herself, *Hopefully Daly will be at his house on the Coast Road by now.*

Herself and Maura had also clashed over Daly and the rumours that he now had a pile of money stuck in a new arcade planned for the headland.

"It could be the making of the place," Maura had proclaimed confidently the previous Sunday.

Catherine returned inside. She had a few odds and ends to tidy in the stores and needed to sort out a box of wafers for later.

"Mark my words, John, hurdy-gurdies will never take off around here," she said confidently as she returned the counter bell to its rightful place.

John paid her no attention and instead banged the side of the fruit machine in frustration.

"Shite!"

Catherine felt her patience ebbing away.

"Go easy there, those things don't grow on trees."

"The bloody thing has me cleaned out," John growled, but he knew better than to attack the machine again.

The muffled sounds of voices and a faint banging downstairs woke Robert Kelly. He had slept in late after the nervous tension of the previous twenty-four hours. There was still a lot to be said to his mother Catherine, but he needed the right time and moment. He glanced around the room. It was like stepping back in time to his childhood, and it was as he had remembered it, unchanged. He had glanced into the dresser drawers before going to bed, and they were, as he had left them ten years previously, untouched, the black tie he had worn to his father's funeral still folded neatly in the bottom drawer.

He could make out the voices of his mother and John Power more clearly now as he climbed out of bed and crossed the faded carpet to take in the view from the small window. The view never failed to disappoint and today was no different, the beach rolling away to the headland on his right, and already there were day trippers dotted along the sand setting up their pitches. Two children were building sandcastles at the water's edge and whooping with excitement as the in-coming waters laid siege to their labours.

In the distance, he could make out the figure of a man and a boy, fishing net in hand, exploring the rock pools. He too had spent many enjoyable hours on the rocks with his father all those years ago. Downstairs, John Power's voice now seemed raised in frustration. He had been a year ahead of Robert in primary school and he had always been a bit of a loner. Robert and his friends had always felt that John Power was a bit "*off*". He had then gone on to the "Tech" in town instead of the brothers and the contact was lost after that, but Robert had recognised him immediately at the fruit machine last night. He hadn't changed in appearance, slightly heavier but still a head of dark wavy curls. Robert scratched a three-day stubble. He needed a shave, and although he knew it would freshen him up, he could do that later. It was time to show his face.

As he descended the stairs, he heard the shop door rattle open and close. Downstairs, his mother was alone:

"The dead arose," she said, shooting him a sideways glance.

"I had forgotten how comfortable that bed was," he answered, not wanting to sound tetchy at being ticked off by his mother after all these years.

"The whole place has gone cuckoo over Jackie Kennedy," she continued.

"It might put the place on the map though and be good for business," Robert answered breezily and quite happy to move the conversation away from his sleeping habits.

"We'll get on just fine, haven't we always," she replied firmly.

There was a silence as Catherine Kelly kept herself active behind the counter, and Robert felt an awkwardness descend that he could not diffuse. Finally, Catherine broke the unease.

"I simply don't understand why you just didn't write. I mean to walk in off the street yesterday like a black stranger."

"I took a notion." His voice sounded restrained.

"After ten years?"

"Am I not welcome?"

"Did you not get my letter that time?"

"I did," he replied curtly.

"And you never thought to answer it," Catherine's probing continued.

"I'm here now."

He had wanted to make contact that time, but he wasn't ready to take control of the business; "make a go of it," as she had put it.

"I had some loose ends to tie up."

"I'll make a pot of tea," she replied, and she moved from behind the counter to the kitchen. He remembered how his mothers' solution to all problems had been to make a cup of tea. Even in their darkest hour, ten years ago, his most abiding memory was copious pots of tea. He heard the kettle whistling, and he found her in the kitchen standing by the table,

"It won't pick up until after two," she said knowingly, placing a neatly arranged tray of cups and teapot on the table. The formality took Robert by surprise, but he took it in his stride. They needed to talk business and he let his mother outline her future for the business; those same plans she had laid out in detail when she had written to him; a transfer of complete ownership to her only son on the one proviso that she could live out her remaining days in the upstairs dwelling. She spoke animatedly about how the business could be developed going forward and how she had put away some funds for the same.

"Just a few pounds to brighten up the place."

Robert could not get a word in edgeways.

"We can sort out the paperwork with O'Flaherty during the week. It's what I've wanted Robert ever since your father..." Her voice trailed off and Catherine blessed herself, took a breath and went to pour herself a fresh cup of tea.

"We could have had all this sorted out if only you had answered my letter, but I suppose there's no use crying over spilled milk," Catherine sighed.

"Well, like you say, you're here now."

Robert looked to change the subject.

"I am and just think what a visit from Jackie Kennedy would do for business," he enthused.

"The publicity that would generate," he added, warming to the task.

"Ah, what is she?" his mother shrugged.

"A chance in a million that would be," he continued unabated, only to be cut off mid-sentence as the counter bell rang out, just once, firmly and loudly.

Scott Scherer took in his surroundings quickly. That was what he was trained to do.

Quaint, he thought to himself, and no immediate threat of danger. He had found the counter bell with little difficulty and had rung it with authority. He allowed himself a smile on spotting the fruit machine in the corner.

Definitely not Vegas.

He admired himself in the mirror. He was looking good, sallow skinned, white teeth and his jet black tightly cut hair swept back with gel. The granite jaw, the one inheritance from his father he was particularly proud of, while his brightly coloured shirt contrasted with the faded surroundings. Prior to this trip his knowledge of Ireland was minimal; some distant relatives and although he had read the brief cover to cover, he always liked to get a physical feel for a place, so he had set off from The Manor to take in the surrounding area in both a professional and personal capacity. The family was having brunch, and it was a period of downtime for the security detail. Scott was happy to have this time alone, and his thoughts consumed him on his leisurely stroll down from The Manor through the village and along the beachfront until he had come across this uninspiring store.

For the first time in months, he felt good about himself, and he appreciated this time to think. He had jumped at the chance to get out of Washington for the week. He needed to get his head straight on what had to be said to his father. He needed to be honest with him and true to himself. He was sure that these few days would be the perfect opportunity to work that out. He promised himself there would be no flirtations here, no one-night stands. Promised himself he would be on his best behaviour; determined to have that conversation with his father once and for all.

He waited at the counter and a woman finally appeared ready to serve:

"Could I have a soda please? Sprite, Ginger ale, whatever."

"Of course," she answered brightly; taking a green bottle from the shelf and placing it on the counter in one fell movement:

"There you go, a *Seven-Up*, that will quench your thirst for you," she said.

"I'm afraid you'll have to bear with me. I haven't fully grasped your Irish pounds, shillings and pence yet," he answered awkwardly, showing her a palm full of coins.

Catherine approached him.

"One of those and two of those lads," she said, picking the coins from his outstretched palm.

"Is it up in The Manor you are?"

"Yes, you could say a working holiday."

"With Mrs. Kennedy?" she asked, placing the coins in the till.

"Actually, that's classified Mam, but I guess there's no harm in saying that Mrs. Kennedy is enjoying her stay here," he continued as Robert Kelly now joined his mother behind the counter; his curiosity getting the better of him on hearing the American accent.

"We have been made to feel very welcome here. In fact, I have some Irish heritage myself, my great-grandmother on my father's side was from *Rauce Coming.*"

"Roscommon," Robert said.

"That's it, *Rauce Coming.*"

"And if there is anything we can do to make your stay more enjoyable, please don't hesitate to ask," Robert added enthusiastically.

Catherine looked at her son quizzically; this pleasantness, catching her somewhat unawares, and at odds with his demeanour since his return home.

"Actually, I was hoping to take John-John for a spot of fishing during the week. Maybe you could recommend some good waters?" the American asked.

"Absolutely, there are some excellent waters around here," Robert replied, coming to the edge of the counter and offering to shake the American's hand.

"Robert Kelly," he offered.

"Scott," the American replied, "Scott Scherer," and the two men exchanged a firm handshake.

Just then the door rattled open, and John Power returned inside, ignoring the two men as he crossed purposefully to the fruit machine. He had unfinished business.

"That would be swell," Scott Scherer answered Robert, but Catherine felt uneasy as John began to play in silence. She had seen his volatility when losing took its grip and often she would encourage him to cut his losses and head home, but it was too early for that yet.

"You can't beat the one-armed man you know. "That sucker has always got something up its sleeve," Scott said in John's general direction and Catherine's heart sank as Scott crossed to stand at John's shoulder. John found this closeness unnerving, especially from someone he had yet to acknowledge.

"That fecking thing," John snarled, coming up short yet again.

"May I?"

"Be my guest," John answered, stepping aside.

Catherine and Robert glanced at each other anxiously at this development, and as Scott struggled momentarily to find the right coins, Catherine felt her anxiety increase. To her surprise and relief, John leaned in, choosing the coins Scott needed.

"There you go," John said softly, placing them in the machine; his own forwardness taking him by surprise. There was a brief silence as both men watched expectantly, but again coming up short.

"Whatever happened to the luck of the Irish," Scott quipped.

"Maybe next time," John answered, and both Catherine and Robert began to relax.

"Maybe," Scott said, leaning in closer and holding out his hand to shake. John paused before taking Scott's hand.

"Scott," the American said confidently. Their eyes met as John mumbled his own name in reply, feeling slightly flushed at this brief exchange.

"I'll take you up on that fishing offer," Scott said breezily as he took his leave with a swagger, closing the door gently behind him.

"Yanks," John snorted, composing himself. "You'd pick them out a mile off."

"Loaded and good for business, though," Robert snapped back quickly.

"One bottle of *Seven-Up* isn't going to break the bank," Catherine said as she returned to the kitchen.

Monday

All day long, John Power had been feeling preoccupied, nervous. He had tried to keep this sense of unease at bay, but no matter how hard he tried the thoughts dominated him, a mixture of fearfulness and a frisson of excitement:

The American.

Had the others noticed anything. Nobody knew. John had always been so mindful to let nothing slip. As far as he was concerned, no one even suspected, but John Power knew that Scott Scherer was not like the others.

This tall dark American.

John tried to dismiss these feelings as his mind playing tricks on him, but now they were back cascading down around him and he felt uneasy again. Catherine was in the stores, and he was alone with the American.

"Shouldn't you be babysitting," John said, starting to play.

"It can wait, if you must know, Daddy stayed on-site today."

"Daddy?" John was curious now.

"Jackie, it's a name me and some of the guys use."

"Like a code."

"Not really, just to cover our asses, really."

"And do they need covering?" John asked.

"We have our moments," Scott said intriguingly.

"More power to ye!" John said, giving the machine a gentle shake.

Scott moved closer.

"I didn't catch your name there yesterday."

"And." John shrugged.

"Are you going to keep me in the dark?"

"Does that bother you?" John said, this time stopping briefly to glance at Scott.

"It interests me," Scott said quietly.

"In that case, you can call me John," he replied, turning to face the screen once more.

"John," Scott said softly. He was standing directly behind John now and John could feel Scott's hot breath on the back of his neck. He smelled good. John felt himself hardening and he didn't resist it; felt his heart beating rapidly as Scott slowly slipped a hand around his waist from behind and felt his erection straining to explode as Scott gently caressed his crotch.

Wednesday

The door rattled open, and Robert Kelly felt that now the timing was right, and he stepped out from behind the counter to confront John Power.

"Is herself about?" John asked.

"No," Robert said sharply.

"Will she be long, do you know? I wanted to see her about something, ask her advice."

"She's busy."

"I'll wait then."

Robert was now standing squarely in the centre of the floor.

"Look, you're not welcome around here," he said.

"Says who?"

"Me, that's who," Robert felt his temper rising.

"On what grounds?"

"Do you want me to spell it out for you?" Robert challenged.

"Yes, I do want you to spell it out for me as a matter of fact," John answered.

"Right so, there's talk."

"What kind of talk?"

"About you and the American," Robert said, blocking John's path aggressively.

"Ah, you have Americans on the brain," John shot back.

"People around here have no truck for that class of thing."

"And what class of thing would that be?"

"Queers."

The word cut through the air like an east wind, but John Power didn't flinch and stayed on the front foot.

"And who made you the spokesperson for people around here all of a sudden?"

"I'll have the final say in this place shortly, and I say…you…loitering around that machine there is a bad image, bad for business."

"I came to see your mother," John said, making to pass him, but Robert grabbed him forcefully by the throat.

"Don't fucking draw me out! You'll be sorry!!" he roared as John brushed his hand away.

Catherine Kelly, who had been busying herself in the kitchen, heard the raised voices and came out to satisfy her curiosity.

"I thought I heard voices," she said.

"I have some news I'd like your opinion on," John said as Robert stepped aside.

"You have."

"Yes. I got talking to the Yank, and he said there's plenty of work for my kind in the States."

"Why, that's fabulous news," Catherine replied.

"Do you think?"

"Of course, a chance in a million."

"And Scott, the Yank, says I could go back with them if I want."

"I couldn't be happier for you, John," Catherine said, brushing past her son to embrace John Power.

"I was anxious to hear what you thought, Catherine. I'd respect your opinion on a matter of this nature."

"And when are you leaving?"

"We are meeting tonight to finalise arrangements. I better be off. I have a million things to do."

"Of course, I can imagine," Catherine said, and the pair hugged one more time as John took his leave.

Catherine and Robert Kelly stood briefly for a moment in silence.

"Isn't that great news. It seems some good will come out of this visit after all," Catherine said.

"Dan Daly was telling me, himself and the Yank had struck up a friendship of sorts."

Catherine glared at her son.

"And when were you in Dan Daly's company?"

"I've spoken to him."

"Have you now."

"Yes."

Robert Kelly strolled back behind the counter, took up a cloth and began an aimless cleaning of anything that took his fancy, waiting for his mothers' response, but there was none. He had more to say and struck while the iron was hot.

"And I don't know what you have against that man either. He only wants what is best for everyone."

"Wants to see us closed more like."

"Nothing could be further from the truth," Robert said, stopping and placing the cloth down on the counter.

"And has he told you this?"

"Yes, he has," he answered firmly, "We have what he needs, access to the beach, but he is prepared to pay a pretty penny for it."

"I'd rather see it rot first," Catherine Kelly bristled. Her son was now leaning on the counter, his eyes fixed on hers.

"Hear me out."

"I've heard enough," she said and made to return to the kitchen.

"Listen, Daly has big plans, mam, lucrative plans, and we can have a say in them, be fully included, properly consulted partners."

"Partners," she answered incredulously.

"Yes, he wants to set this place up as the top resort in the whole South East, and he has the finances to do it. He will have tourists flocking in, an Amusement Arcade on the headland with carousels and a boating lake. A Hypermarket with shopping and trolleys.

"Hypermarket? Trolleys? Tis soft in the head, you are gone," Catherine huffed, throwing her eyes up to heaven in disgust.

"And with our right of way we could have a caravan park adjacent to the beach, the best of both worlds," Robert was animated now, standing tall behind the counter, and Catherine was taken aback at the enthusiasm she could see on her son's face.

"No," was all she could muster in reply, but Robert was in full flow.

"A burger bar on site serving the holidaymakers and day trippers."

"Burgers…here?"

"With fries, cooked American style, a lick of paint here, a few stars and stripes there."

"Over my dead body," Catherine said. She was angry now at her son's flight of fancy, but there was no quelling, Robert.

"You don't get it, Mam, working with him. He will pay big money for access to set up the caravan site as part of the overall development plan. We'd have the franchise on The American Diner, and who's to say in a few years' time we won't have them dotted along the coast in every resort from here to Rosslare."

"No."

"If we don't take this opportunity, someone else will, trust me."

"Jesus Christ, boy, I said no!"

John Power loved the view from the headland. He scanned the bay as a gentle July breeze swirled around him. He needed cooling. He felt flushed once more. In the distance he could make out Kelly's. Looking at the store from this perspective always fascinated him. He thought of how by the end of the week, this view would be but a distant memory; perhaps even a source of solace for him during the early weeks of adjustment. He felt some feelings of trepidation, but that was why he had chosen this spot. It was a place of sanctuary and held many memories. He had often come here over the years when he felt confused or wracked with guilt. It was here he would come to reconcile himself with what he was; what he had become. From here he could see everything, everyone. It was here he had come with Paul Daly that first time, two twelve-year-olds.

A bit of messing.

He had often met Paul after, but it was never mentioned; their shared secret, and now he'd see him in town with his wife and two kids. Their eyes never met.

Scott was also gazing into middle-distance, and he seemed miles off.

"You're quiet," John said.

"Just thinking."

"What about? Us?"

"This and that."

John took a step back from the cliff edge and sat on one of the moss-covered ledges that dotted the headland. Overhead, seagulls cackled and cawed, circling a shoal of Pollock breaking off the shore below.

"Is it true what they say?" John mused aloud.

"What?"

"That there is a place in the U.S. and fellas like us."

"Gay," Scott interrupted him.

"Yeah."

"Say it, then," Scott said, raising his voice slightly.

John paused and took a breath; Scott's tone took him by surprise.

"…Gays, like you and me, can go and get married," John felt a dryness in his throat.

"If you are that way inclined," Scott answered, calmer now.

"Would you?"

"What?"

"Get married to a gay."

"Jesus Christ! What are you going on about!" This time, there was no mistaking Scott's tone.

"Me and you," John said.

"Me and you!! Just slow down a damn second. We had some fun alright. Let's just leave it at that."

"Jesus, you don't have to eat me. I was only saying. Christ!!" John answered.

"Well now you've said it."

"Ok, we'll just keep it as we are, so. See how it goes when we get there," John said, trying to diffuse the atmosphere.

Scott bristled once more.

"Fucking hell. Hang on a minute. We are not going anywhere, me and you."

"But you told me you'd fix it up, arrange it."

"I told you what you wanted to hear," Scott wasn't even looking at John now, and John felt a rush of desperation come over him.

"No…no Scott, you said you had contacts."

Scott laughed.

"Play the game now John, what we done, you wanted it."

"Yes, of course," John answered.

"I never forced you or anything."

"No."

"A willing, consenting partner, enjoyed it too."

"Yes, but I thought there was more…is more."

This time, Scott did address John directly.

"You didn't seriously think for one second I was going to bring you with me back to the States!"

"But I did, Scott, yes."

Scott advanced on John aggressively before stopping short.

"Come off it. What kind of putz do you take me for? You, got what you wanted."

John Power felt his old life slipping away from him, a life he had guarded for fifteen years. Desperation overwhelmed him.

"You don't get it. I can't live here now."

"Leave then," Scott said, "But get one thing straight, I'm not your meal ticket."

"This will finish me," John pleaded, but he knew it was in vain.

"I'm going to the pub," Scott said, "Now are you coming or not." And he made his way down the headland.

※

Catherine Kelly had closed early. She didn't have the stomach for it today. A silence had descended, and Robert had taken to his room.

Partners with Dan Daly...My God, the man who codded his father up to his eyeballs that time.

She pottered around the kitchen confused and the memories came flooding back; of how Dan Daly and her husband Frank had gone in as partners to buy up that site on the headland in the first place and how Frank had lost the family savings, every cent. And now this; over her dead body, this time. She heard the bedroom door open and her son descending the stairs. Robert stood in the jamb of the kitchen door:

"Is that your final word on it, so?"

Catherine didn't answer.

"There's no talking to you," Robert said.

"Partners with him! Jesus Christ, young fella! Have you no shame at all? Is that what they taught you in London?

Robert shrugged.

"Your father lost a fortune that time."

"Daly bought out Dad's share."

"That deal killed your father, drove him over the edge, to do what he done. Your father is lying beyond the boundary wall of his parish graveyard, and as far as I'm concerned, Dan fucking Daly put him there. He might as well have pushed him off those rocks himself."

"Corner shops are called in mam," Robert said, but he didn't recognise his mother anymore; what his mild-mannered mother had become.

Dan fucking Daly.

She was transformed before his eyes and he knew at that moment there was no turning back; knew, although she hadn't spelled it out, that there would be no trip to Flaherty the solicitor.

John Power felt cold now. The sun had dipped beyond the horizon and the sea had turned an ominous grey. He stood up and felt a tightness in his stomach.

Panic-stricken.

A terror seized him. What had he done?

You couldn't believe daylight out of Americans.

He'd be a laughingstock now. A life he had protected diligently was slipping like sand through his grasp. Scott's words had cut him. The coldness.

Dismissiveness.

He felt himself swaying. Lightheaded. His stomach felt nauseous. It overwhelmed him. How had he been so stupid; so blindsided? Terror gripped him. He couldn't face the locals. The ridicule.

"Jesus!" he shouted and began to weep.

The confusion.

He stepped closer to the edge. Below him, the silver bellied Pollock glistened. He didn't feel present anymore, didn't feel anything. Numb.

You got what you wanted. Enjoyed it.

And now he could no longer see the bay. He retched, and he thought again of Paul Daly all those years ago; of how he had made a family life for himself instead of the dirty little world John inhabited. Two hundred feet below him the sea had changed, and the waves were gathering apace. John Power stood transfixed. He needed to be free, and he could no longer see such freedom in tomorrow.

He stepped forward….

Saturday

Catherine Kelly stepped out of the kitchen. She was dressed in black from head to toe, and it brought her back to another funeral.

"Am I alright?" she asked.

"Fine altogether," Maura answered as she fought to remain composed.

"I haven't worn this since…" Catherine's voice trailed off.

"We should be going if we want to make the church on time," Maura said.

"'Tis good of you to come with me. I appreciate it."

"You're the brave one. It's the least I could do."

"I'd have to for John," Catherine said.

"Fr O'Sullivan had the workmen above there all day yesterday, knocked the old boundary wall and put a walkway through to where the new plots will be. He was having the bishop down early today to bless the land," Maura said.

"So, my Frank finally gets to rest in peace."

"Circumstances change Catherine. Fr O'Sullivan wanted to address it, and now with this, John-business."

Robert Kelly joined his mother behind the counter.

"Are you going to the funeral yourself?" Maura asked him.

"I can't. I must catch the bus into town and then on to Rosslare for this evening's ferry."

Maura couldn't hide her surprise: "You're leaving."

"I am. There's nothing to keep me here now. There'll be no development on the headland now after what's happened. A stigma like that will be hard to shake off. People have awful long memories."

"And Jackie Kennedy has upped and left us too. Cut her visit short, didn't want to be caught up in the fuss, with John's funeral," Maura said.

Catherine Kelly came out from behind the counter and walked slowly to the fruit machine. She unplugged it.

"I was sure this old thing would be the death of him. Did you know I was reading that you can get a tennis game now where two can play each other, and it costs a shilling a game," she said.

"A shilling to play a game. What's the world coming too," Maura said.

"I was thinking maybe I should get one in as a replacement."

"Do you think it will catch on?" Maura asked.

"The Yanks wouldn't be making them if people weren't paying the money".

Robert Kelly shifted uneasily: "I'll probably be gone when you get back."

"You'll write, won't you," Catherine said.

"I will," Robert replied, returning upstairs to leave the two women alone in silence.

"There'll be no arcade now. The talk is Dan Daly is going to invest in a mobile burger van," Maura said eventually.

"Burgers no less," Catherine sighed.

"He will be able to service all the big matches, race meetings and even bring it to Tramore or Wexford for the day."

"I see."

"The son Paul is going in with him. He has head screwed on that fella."

"Himself and John were pals one time," Catherine said.

"Daly was saying there'd be work for me. If you don't mind, that is. He pays well."

"I don't," Catherine said."

I couldn't look a gift horse like that in the mouth."

"Certainly not," Catherine answered.

The two women walked out into the cooling July air.

"There's a fierce change in it," Maura said, pulling her coat tightly around herself.

"There is," Catherine answered.

"And what are you going to do now?" Maura asked.

"What I always did," Catherine said, linking Maura as the two women made their way to the Church.

Scott Scherer eased himself into his seat as flight EI7036 taxied down the runway at Shannon Airport. The pilot was in charge now, and to his left the young boy John was already starting to doze. Scott closed his eyes. His mind was made up; he would contact his father as soon as he was back on American soil. He would sit him down and spell out clearly what his intentions were going forward. He couldn't go on living like this, furtive meetings with casual acquaintances. He had dodged a bullet this time, and he wanted something more. He would move to San Francisco and make a go of it there with like-minded people. As the plane began to ascend, he took one last look at the Emerald Isle. He had never gotten to take the young boy fishing after all. Scott Scherer settled himself as sleep took hold. He had asked the stewardess to wake him for the food. He looked to his left one more time. Across the aisle, the boy was sleeping soundly.

Prisoners Dilemma

Detective Sergeant Sean Breen had taken off his watch and was shaking it vigorously. Almost thirty years of experience on the job and the one thing that still completely threw him was not having the proper time.

"Fuck it," he cursed aloud.

Garda Susan Keogh watched him closely, but she didn't feel it her place to pass any comment. She had been warned about Breen; told that he was difficult, but this was an opportunity too good to turn down for the young guard straight out of training college. Susan Keogh had made her mind up. She was prepared to put up with Breen's notorious brusqueness if it meant getting a foothold in the force. Keogh was ambitious and if placating an old dinosaur like Breen had to be done, she was prepared to do it.

"What time is it now?" he finally asked.

"Quarter past," Keogh answered. "Is the battery gone or something?"

"Just go out and see if he is here yet," Breen said as he put the offending watch back on his wrist.

Susan Keogh knew she better do as she was told, and she made to leave to follow through on Breen's request.

"You'll be strictly observing right. I'll take the lead. There's going to be some hard questions to be asked," Breen said as Susan reached the door.

"I'm well aware of what needs to be done," Susan Keogh bristled.

"Walsh's daughter has just disappeared off the face of the earth, and I don't want you barging in with some bullshit fresh out of Templemore."

"Right Sarge," she said.

"And that's Detective Sergeant to you," Breen added.

Susan Keogh bit her lip. It was a nervous habit she had developed when she felt her emotions getting the better of her. She was determined not to blow this big chance the first day.

"It will be strictly by the book," she said firmly.

"Good, I'm twenty-seven years at this caper, so I must be doing something right. What time is the friend due in?"

"Aisling O'Connor."

"Yeah, the O'Connor girl."

"Four."

"We'll keep it nice and casual. Routine questioning. We don't want anyone getting spooked."

This time, Susan Keogh could not contain herself:

"I have done interviews before, you know."

"How many?" Breen shot back.

"Pardon."

"You heard me, how many? How many fucking interviews, one, two, ten, more than ten, more than twenty?"

Susan Keogh was struggling to keep her rage in check:

"I know the procedure."

"Look, you're still a rookie. You watch. You learn, and you speak when you're spoken to."

"You can't talk to me like that."

"Write me up," Breen snapped. "I want closure on this. These stories get legs, and the last thing we need is some wise guy down from the *Sunday Independent* doing a piece on serial killers and comparing the town to *Bad Day at* fucking *Blackrock*!"

"Do you want my gut feeling on it?" she asked Breen.

"Not particularly."

"I'd say she's a dead duck."

"Would you now."

"Yes."

"Six weeks in the job and you've deduced all this without a shred of evidence, amazing-fucking amazing."

"Call it feminine intuition."

"And did it ever cross your mind that this girl Sinead might not want to be found?"

"To be honest with you, no," she replied.

"Well, we will be pursuing every possible angle and making our deductions from proper detective work. Now don't let the door hit you on the way out."

Prick.

This was going to be more difficult than Susan had first envisaged. She walked to the reception area, composing herself as she went. She couldn't show any emotion to the girl's father. She knew first impressions were a vital part of detective work. Emotion was the enemy and would cloud judgement.

"Mr. Walsh?"

Paul Walsh's heart sank. The previous twenty-four hours had been a living nightmare. He hadn't slept, worry consumed him, and first impressions were that this young female guard did not inspire confidence. He needed reassurance. He followed her down the corridor, his mind a complete blur, as she showed him into a small windowless room. The air smelled dank, and Sean Breen was seated at a small table underneath a sharp bright light.

"Take a seat Paul…good of you to come. It must be difficult for you," Breen said, and Walsh briefly acknowledged Breen as he sat at the table. The young guard also took a seat opposite.

"How are you bearing up?" Breen asked.

"It's hard to describe the feeling…the not knowing and no trace of her. That's what's killing me."

"And has anything come to mind? Something out of the ordinary," Breen asked.

"No."

"You see, what we are trying to do at this early stage is build up a picture of her last few hours that we know of. To be honest, we are having difficulty nailing down specific times. So, anything you can give would be a help," Breen said.

"Do you think my girl is still alive?" Paul Walsh asked.

Breen glanced at Susan Keogh, and she was surprised, as for the first time her senior colleague seemed at a loss for words.

"Don't fucking mess me about on this," Paul Walsh continued.

Breen shifted some papers uneasily on the table as Keogh watched him closely. Finally, he spoke:

"It's a hard call, but you have my word. No one will mess anyone about."

"And how would you describe your daughter, Mr. Walsh?" Susan Keogh asked, a question that drew a glare from Breen at her side.

"Life couldn't have been better for her really," Paul Walsh said as he took out his wallet, removed a photo and slid it across the table to the young guard. Susan Keogh examined the photo of his smiling, vibrant daughter with her blonde highlighted hair swept back and her pearl drop earrings sparkling in the sun.

"She is beautiful," she said.

"She was…is," Walsh replied, trying to fight the onset of tears.

Sean Breen took the photograph, placed it in front of himself on the table and looked at it studiously before speaking:

"It's a good likeness. Do you mind if we run some copies of it? This could be useful."

Paul Walsh nodded.

"And her mood this last few weeks, was she happy?" Susan Keogh asked, ignoring the icy stare from Breen.

"Everything was going for her. Just back to take up her place in college next month," Walsh answered.

"Do you know if she was in a relationship?" Susan continued, but this time Breen raised his hand across her to cut her off:

"Let's not be running away with ourselves, shall we? Her last sighting was when she left the dental appointment at quarter to five. Is that correct?"

"Yes, she would have been heading home at that stage, and I normally get in from work about half past."

Susan Keogh took the hint from Breen, and she eased back into her chair, listening intently as Paul Walsh outlined a picture of his only daughter Sinead, who had recently returned from a gap year in Boston to take up her college offer from the previous summer. She watched the tears well up as he explained how these last few weeks had been an opportunity for father and daughter to reconnect and for Sinead to make up for lost time with her younger brother, something which she had embraced fully.

"The house had laughter again."

All the while, she noted how Sean Breen sat impassively as Walsh spoke, allowing him the time to fill in more detail of how she had met a boy from Mayo in Boston, a hospital worker Terry Donnelly, but that Walsh knew little of him. The boy was due home for Christmas, and Sinead had briefly mentioned that he might come on a visit. He didn't know how serious it was:

"You know them at that age."

Susan Keogh made a few cursory notes as Walsh spoke, nothing specific, a show of professionalism more for Breen than anything else.

"Was there any particular reason why she went to Boston that time?" she asked eventually as Walsh took a breath.

"She wanted to see the world a bit, get the travel bug out of her system."

"And did you mind her deferring college like that?" she continued as Walsh took a moment to gather his thoughts.

"I…we missed her."

"So, there was no inkling whatsoever that something was amiss," she said.

"No, 'tis completely out of character for her to go and do something like this of her own accord."

Breen took control:

"What we would like you to do for us is to check her personal details, bank account, passport, that sort of thing. Will you be able to do that? It's just we need an open mind on all fronts."

There was a brief silence before Paul Walsh stood:

"Is that all?"

Susan Keogh felt the dynamic in the room shift, but she could not put her finger on it exactly. She looked towards Breen for a response. He appeared unruffled as Walsh turned to leave the room.

"For the time being. Will you get back to us as quickly as you can with those details?" Breen said.

"I will," Walsh answered, no longer looking before stopping briefly at the door. Susan Keogh also stood quickly, remembering that it was her duty to see Walsh out of the station.

"How would you describe your own relationship with her?" Breen asked almost nonchalantly.

"Pardon," Walsh answered, turning to face the table again.

"How did ye get on?"

"I don't get your meaning exactly," Walsh said. Susan Keogh looked at both men.

"Simple enough question, really. She would have been around eight or nine by the time her brother was born. She'd have a clear enough recollection of that."

"That was a long time ago," Walsh replied sharply, and Susan Keogh could feel an escalation in hostility between the two men.

"I have a good memory of it," Breen said.

Slowly, Walsh returned to the table and placed both his hands on it:

"I don't like your inference."

Susan Keogh studied Breen for a reaction, but his face betrayed nothing.

"I'll be more specific. Do you think Sinead held any grudges against you over that business with her mother?"

Walsh banged the table with the palm of his hand, and Susan Keogh could feel her own heart rate rising.

"No! She never saw that, and it was never spoken of after," Walsh said.

Breen didn't flinch and began to tidy the documents on the table:

"She grew up in the house," he said.

"You won't throw that in my face, Breen. That was between me and Angela, God rest her. We made our peace."

"Can you detail your own movements last night after four thirty?" Breen asked.

Walsh turned away in anger and walked to the door: "I don't have to listen to this."

"Can you go through your movements last night?" This time Breen was firm and forceful.

"Yes," Walsh snapped back, opened the door quickly and left the room. Susan Keogh went to follow him, but Breen gestured at her to remain:

"Let him go and shut that door."

Susan Keogh did as she was told.

"What the fuck do you think you are playing at? I'm the senior officer here and I'm running this fucking investigation. Putting ideas in his head about some poor bastard living in Boston, for Christ's sake!" Breen said, making no attempt to conceal his anger. Susan Keogh felt herself quivering but knew now was not the time to show any signs of weakness.

"And there's no problem with you practically accusing the man himself of it. What kind of line of questioning is that?"

"I have a lever on Walsh ok, so I threw it at him to see what would happen. The man was a wife beater alright, so who knows, maybe he roughed up his daughter, and it got out of hand."

"And you never thought to share that information with me, to keep me in the loop."

"It slipped my mind."

"Tell me about Walsh," she said firmly, pulling out the chair to sit opposite Breen. He sat slowly back in his chair and explained how Walsh's wife had died four years earlier through "drink and fear" and that the young girl Sinead had kept the family together. There had been one serious domestic when Angela was pregnant with the boy and Breen been called to the home that night:

"I wanted to take him outside and sort him myself."

"And after?" Susan asked.

"She didn't press charges and he kept his nose clean. That was the only time we were involved."

The room fell silent.

"Angela was a quiet dignified woman who suffered in silence," Breen said, gathering up his papers before standing up:

"Now you know," he said.

"Do you think he has it in him to hurt his daughter?" Susan asked.

"I know for a fact he is a difficult man to live with."

"But murder…"

"Steady now, girl, let's not go putting the cart before the horse. We keep an open mind, and our interview strategy will be the *prisoner's dilemma* approach."

"Now who is talking Templemore bullshit," she said.

"The oldest trick in the book, girl. We talk to all the major players on a one-to-one basis and set one conversation against the other. A picture will emerge. I guarantee it."

"So, we are going to work together then."

For the first time all morning, Breen allowed himself a brief smile and reminded Susan Keogh of her father.

Detective Sergeant Barry Keogh had served the force with distinction before making the ultimate sacrifice, gunned down on security detail outside *St Paul's* Credit Union. Susan had worshipped the ground he walked upon. Her earliest memory was sitting on the side of the bath as a young child watching him shave. It fascinated her. He had a special mug for lathering the soap and he was meticulous. She had a clear memory that she carried with her of asking him one morning about how he was going to spend his day, and the answer that stayed with her:

"I'll try and help a few people."

He made it sound so simple and such a natural thing to want to do. Initially, she had met some familial resistance to her wish to follow in her father's footsteps, but she had a stubborn streak and knew deep down she could make him proud, deep down that maybe she could make a difference also. At training college, she didn't want preferential treatment. She wanted to emulate him, but she didn't want it easy. Her father losing his life in the line of duty was never mentioned and not spoken of when she was assigned to the station, but she knew Breen knew. She was happy to work with him. She felt if she could hack it with Breen, she could hack it with anyone. She felt better about the interview process now.

Prisoners Dilemma.

She felt the air had been cleared between them. Now it was a waiting game to hear what the friend had to say.

※

Aisling O'Connor was nervous. She had never been inside a Garda station before. The young female guard seemed pleasant and had shown her to the room to wait. She scanned the walls; a couple of *Neighbourhood Watch security* posters and a few *COVID-19* posters also prominent. The last couple of hours had been a complete blur. She had left a couple of voice messages, all unanswered, on Sinead's phone. They had been due to meet at *The Sportsman* for a chat and a few drinks. She knew after ten minutes. Sinead was a stickler for time and always had been, ever since Primary School. None of this made sense:

"She told me everything," Aisling explained to the two Garda when they joined her in the room.

"What kind of things?" the male asked.

"Girls, stuff."

"Would you say this disappearance is totally out of character?" he continued.

"Yes, she didn't run away. Not Sinead."

"Did she talk much about her new boyfriend at all-the lad she met in Boston?" the female guard asked.

"A bit."

"Would you say it was serious?" she continued.

"I never met him," Aisling replied.

"Did she say much about Boston in general?" the female guard asked.

"I suppose."

"Were you surprised at all that she went out there that time?"

"It came out of the blue a bit, yes."

"Do you think there was a particular reason?"

Breen interjected before Aisling O'Connor could answer:

"Her father indicated that she might have needed her space. Does that make sense to you?"

Aisling O'Connor avoided eye contact with the two Garda:

"That was probably it."

"Would that have been something ye talked about?" Breen asked.

"I think there was something she wanted, was coming round to tell me."

"And you have no idea what," the female guard said.

"No. I think that's why she wanted to meet me last night. Boston just struck me as…trying to get away."

There was a silence as both Garda looked to process what Aisling O'Connor had just suggested.

"From what?" Susan Keogh asked eventually.

"Something. I don't know."

"Or somebody-maybe?"

"Maybe. Will you find her?" Aisling O'Connor asked.

"We hope so," Breen said.

The chat had run its course, and both guards walked Aisling O'Connor out of the station.

"Well?" Breen asked as they watched her leave.

"She knows something," Susan Keogh said quietly.

She was sure of it.

※

"Sinead was pregnant."

Susan Keogh left the words hanging in the air. She had felt an expectant buzz all morning, right from the moment Aisling O'Connor had made contact. It was Susan who had suggested this coffee shop away from the formality of the station. Across from them two elderly ladies were engrossed in conversation. Susan remained calm and took a slow sip from her cup. She didn't want to spook Aisling O'Connor:

"The guy from Mayo," she said, placing her cup down gently.

"No, before she went to the States."

"Did she tell you who the father was?"

"She wouldn't say."

"And did her father know?"

"I'm not sure. All she said was that it would be a scandal if it came out."

"Was she looking for advice?"

"No, she had her mind made up on going to America to have the child."

"Not for an abortion."

"God no."

"And then?"

"To give it up for adoption. She had it all worked out."

Susan Keogh could see the relief in Aisling O'Connor's face as the two women continued to chat; Susan explaining that she would have to run this new information by her commanding officer, as the investigation would have to run by the book.

"A formal statement may be warranted. Will you be ok with that?" Susan asked as the two women parted company in the street. Aisling O'Connor nodded and shook her hand, and Susan Keogh headed back to the station. She wondered what Breen would make of it all.

Breen exhaled: "Good work."

"I'd like another crack at her," Susan said, but Breen quickly put a dampener on her enthusiasm:

"We'll see how it pans out. It could be just a vivid imagination."

Susan Keogh was disappointed. She felt she was close, but Breen appeared nonplussed.

"Is it time to trace the boyfriend?" she asked.

"Leave that to me."

"What about Walsh? He must have known."

"Not necessarily."

"Come on. You mean to tell me if one of your daughters was pregnant you wouldn't twig it."

"Ain't got no daughters or sons either, just me and the wife and no parental stress. Look, we'll get Walsh in for an update, but when he does come in, we'll keep this pregnancy business in reserve for the time being alright."

Susan Keogh didn't respond.

"I said alright."

"Yes, boss," she replied grudgingly.

Susan Keogh felt frustrated. Paul Walsh was already ten minutes at the station, and she felt the general chit-chat was serving no purpose.

What was Breen playing at?

Walsh hadn't shaved, and his eyes looked tired. Breen was fidgeting distractedly with his watch again.

Was this a tactic?

She fought to contain herself.

"Have ye actually any real news for me?" Walsh finally asked.

Breen slowly and deliberately placed the watch back on his wrist:

"In fact, some information has come to light."

Susan Keogh felt her heart skip a beat.

"What kind of information?" Walsh asked.

"We can't divulge it. We need to clarify certain…aspects," Breen said, looking directly at Walsh as he spoke.

"It's my daughter, for Christ's sake!"

Susan felt the urge to speak, to reassure, but Breen's glare had *not now* written all over it. Walsh composed himself:

"Is she safe?"

"We are still working on the premise that Sinead is out there," Breen answered.

"Alive?"

"This is not a murder investigation," Breen answered.

Susan Keogh could feel Walsh's eyes on her now. He was looking for a reaction, but she averted his gaze; hoping against hope that her face would not betray her own feelings on the matter.

Walsh spoke calmly as he stood from the table:

"I want it on record, my objection to the way you are running this investigation, and I want that written down," he said, pointing forcefully at Susan Keogh.

"Sit down," Breen said, but Walsh remained unmoved.

"Sit down, Mr. Walsh," Susan Keogh said, gesturing towards the empty chair.

"I have nothing more to say," he answered.

"In that case, just one last thing…show me your arms," Breen asked.

"What?"

"Your arms. Show me them."

"Fuck you," Walsh spat out, his eyes dancing with rage, but Breen did not flinch:

"Are you going to show them to me or am I going to have to make you do it."

Walsh rolled up his sleeves in an angry gesture:

"There...satisfied."

Breen examined both arms in an exaggerated manner:

"Yes, and now you can go."

Walsh left the room, crashing the door shut behind him. Now it was Susan Keogh's turn to let fly:

"What are you playing at? So, he has no marks on his arms! What does that prove? Only pisses him off further. I mean…show me your arms," she demanded.

"Now you are starting to annoy me, good and proper." Breen answered.

"And now you know what he felt like, go on, show them."

Breen raised his arms over his head to expose both forearms.

"And you could be going away to get a battery for that watch at this stage!" Keogh said.

"You cheeky bitch!" Breen laughed. "It must have been someone she knew when she didn't resist, ok, now fuck off!!"

Susan Keogh gathered up her notes and strolled back to her desk. A thousand thoughts raced through her mind; What would Terry Donnelly have to say for himself? Was there someone Sinead was having difficulty trying to shake off? Was there someone giving her a hard time?

It must have been someone she knew when she didn't resist.

She made herself a cup of coffee. She thought a walk might help, but the thoughts wouldn't subside. It was bugging her, and it remained with her throughout the rest of the day.

Susan Keogh had slept fitfully, adrenaline coursing through her body all night. Occasionally, she had turned on the bedside lamp to jot down some notes, fearing that her thought process would be forgotten by morning. It was daylight now and she swung the curtains open to the sounds of birdsong. She lay on the bed, counting the clock down to six thirty am. That would be a reasonable hour.

Where would she start?

She flicked through the array of post-it's on her bedside locker.

Walsh-he was hard to live with.

It must have been someone she knew when she didn't resist.

She was meeting Breen for a review at ten.

"You said you knew for a fact that Walsh was hard to live with."

"I sure did," Breen answered.

"But and this has been bugging me since yesterday… How do you know that, though-for a fact, I mean?"

Breen sat back in his chair confidently:

"That's why they pay me the big money."

"Or…unless…someone told you."

"What are you getting at exactly?" Breen replied, sitting forward once more, as Keogh fought the urge to bite her lip:

"Just trying to piece it together in my head," she said.

"Try me."

"You didn't mention the possibility that Sinead was pregnant to Walsh. Why was that?"

"Hearsay, nothing to be gained by it. Haven't I taught you anything these last few days? Hard evidence, girl, that's what gets the job done."

"And then you said…," Keogh checked her notes. "It must have been someone she knew when she didn't resist."

"So."

"And she didn't resist…did she? Nobody could call it that close…unless…unless they were there themselves," she said calmly.

"What are you implying?"

"Looking, listening, learning. Like you told me, day one."

Breen, almost imperceptibly, shifted slightly in his chair:

"Talking shite, more like."

"No," she said firmly:

"You-you were there-that's how you know she didn't resist."

The words were out. She had said it. What had kept her awake until the small hours, ruminated on through the night, and she had never felt so relaxed, nerveless. Her eyes remained focused on Breen, and she studied him as the colour drained from his face: his eyes telling their own story:

"Are you joking me! That's the most ridiculous thing I ever heard!!" Breen began to laugh, and he swung back into his chair forcefully.

"I'm right, though, aren't I…she didn't resist…Only someone who saw it would say that. You said it yourself. It must have been someone she knew. You knew her didn't you-not just as Walsh's daughter, knew her more than that, knew for a fact Walsh was a prick to live with because Sinead told you."

"Christ, stop it! enough woman!" And before her very eyes Detective Sergeant Sean Breen began to unravel, crumble like the pieces of a jigsaw back into their box, only this was a dismantling of a different nature, a shrinking to the truth.

"Jesus, you were there."

"I just wanted to talk to her, explain, but there was no getting through to her."

"Jesus-What's after happening, sergeant?" Keogh asked, betraying no emotion and the truth trickled forth, slowly at first and then cascaded into an unstoppable wave, how Breen had been flattered at first by the attentions of this young girl before fantasies gave way to lust and then had it all arranged that Sinead would go to America to have the child and put it up for adoption:

"Nobody would have been any the wiser. That's the great thing about this job. You will always know someone. Have some backdoor somewhere, a doctor, solicitor, priest-somebody. It all works on favours," Breen said quietly.

"Your baby."

"Isn't that a funny thing? Catherine and I couldn't have a child of our own. Adoption was mentioned at one stage, but she was not switched on to it. A bit like Sinead in the end."

"She wanted to keep the baby," Susan Keogh was slowly piecing the jigsaw back together.

"Not to begin with. At first, everything went according to plan, but, when the child was born, she couldn't give it up. Moved in with Donnelly, herself and the baby."

"I see."

"Came home then with mad talk of going to college and moving in with this Donnelly fella as a couple with my son. I couldn't let that happen..." his voice trailed off.

"So, you killed her instead."

Breen threw his arms in the air:

"It wasn't like that. I just wanted her to see sense. That would have been the end of me. It was an accident."

"Where will we find her?"

Breen tore a page from his own notebook, wrote on it quickly, and passed the page across the table to his young colleague:

"There you go…case closed." he said before removing his watch and setting it down in the middle of the table:

"You will need it for evidence. It took a knock when I struck her."

Breen stared impassively into middle-distance before the tears began to form, but Susan Keogh felt nothing. She knew what she had to do; set up a formal interview and bag the evidence properly. She also knew that her father would be proud of her. She was doing good for someone, helping a girl who could no longer help herself.

Prisoners Dilemma.

Listening to the conversations and seeing where they took you. The oldest trick in the book.

The Invisible Boy

They said my father was fond of it and that it killed him in the end. Said he drank his redundancy from Fords and spent all his days in The Tavern.

"Fuck em!"

I remember that differently. We always had food on the table, never wanted anything and not once was there ever an angry word or even a hint of him raising a glove to us or me mam. That's how I remember it and when she passed that's what broke him in the end, what he couldn't cope with. That once again his life had been turned upside down, this time his soul mate, and just like before, there was absolutely nothing he could do about it. And I also remember how at this second time of asking there was also a difference, an impending finality to it, a realisation that his life was running its course on empty. He soldiered on, but he was ready after that, had nothing to live for, and he didn't want to be hanging around, be a burden to anyone. The neighbours didn't see that and of course he never said it straight out, never told me for sure, but I could see it in his face, read it in his movements. The glue was gone.

Sometimes he'd let the mask slip.

"'Tis all going through life," he'd say.

Not often, maybe once or twice a year and that was it. And I'd never bring it up about herself or Michael.

The brother was ten years older than me and gave me a good grounding in what he was most passionate about, music, and so while all my classmates were listening to *The Bay City Rollers* and wondering when I was going to adjust my trousers tartan appropriately, I was into *Bowie* and *Slade*. Nothing was off limits to my nine-year-old self on this musical educational journey; *The Who*; *Live at Leeds*, *Jethro Tull*, *Johnny Winter*, *Deep Purple*, and *Mike Oldfield* all got an airing while the long-suffering parents showed tremendous patience as the sounds from the latest vinyl offerings reverberated around the house or as *Noddy Holder's* high-pitched holler crackled around the bedroom late at night from *Radio Luxembourg*. All this ended one glorious June bank Holiday Weekend when Michael came off his motorbike heading to see *Rory Gallagher* at the Mountain Dew Festival in Macroom. I answered the door and I remember seeing the parish priest, a guard and Michael's boss from work. Straight away, I knew it wasn't right. I remember my mother took a turn, a weakness, and I can still see the men propping her up at the kitchen sink-screaming-hysterical, as I was ushered into the good room.

Michael was rarely spoken about after, and that night was never mentioned again.

"That was awful what happened," the neighbours said.

"Shur, you'd never get over that."

And I became Michael Ryan's brother, the invisible boy.

The evening of the funeral, I was sent to The Tavern to find my father. He had escaped there with his brother, a refuge from a house of pain. My first time inside the doors and the casual drinkers nodding knowingly in my direction.

Michael Ryan's brother.

I found them in the lounge. I had never seen my father drunk before, seen him cry. Back at the house, relatives put him to bed, saying:

"He needed that, to get it out of his system."

Mam wore black for a year, numbed, and often took to the bed for days when reality kicked in.

I took it upon myself to protect them from the grim and grey outside world of the 70s, swiftly changing TV channels at the first hint of tragedy and combing the newspaper for any stories that might cause distress on long, slow walks home from the corner shop. We were enveloped in a sadness that there was no escape from. The day of the *Miami Showband* massacre, there was no hiding place from grief; my mother cried bitterly while he cut the hedges in silence, and I couldn't understand how they could both exhibit such anguish for people they didn't even know.

My father, to his eternal credit, tried as best he could, and walked me to *Woolworths* for my copy of *Telegram Sam.* I can still see the blue label with the red silhouette of *Marc Bolan*, but it didn't feel right.

"Turn that down a touch, boy…your mother is sleeping."

The day the music died.

I kept my head down, not wanting to cause them any more grief. Exams were passed, school and college, but they had lost the gift of celebrating even my most meagre achievements. What Michael had lost out on consumed them and while I hadn't realised it at the time, my life had changed too that Bank Holiday weekend. The joy was gone, and I dedicated myself to doing what I thought was right by them. Dedicated myself to giving them stability and a quiet life. Guilt wouldn't allow it any other way.

When my chance did come to fly the coop, I blew it. Her name was Rachel, and we had been introduced by acquaintances who felt the timing was perfect; she returned from an emotionally bruising experience in London and me plodding along.

"In a rut," they said.

At first, they both appeared happy for me, but they couldn't enjoy my life, our lives, or make any emotional attachment to us as a couple. Rachel found this fragility difficult, felt I needed saving from my own parents, and suggested that we make some time for ourselves. So, we took a chance and headed to Australia for a year. Two months in, the news broke:

"Your mother got some bad news."

There was a silence on the end of the line that said it all:

"We didn't want you to be worrying about it being so far away and all, but…"

Duty called.

I didn't want to be seen to be gallivanting on the other side of the world and didn't want it to be all about me, so Rachel acquiesced. She made all the right noises; felt I'd regret it if I didn't return and let me decide to do what I was conditioned for.

"I fully understand," was her verdict.

I flew back within the week, and it was a short six months putting my shoulder to the wheel. Rachel is settled in Melbourne now with a lawyer and three kids, the last I heard.

He went downhill fast after mam died and within the year his life had been reduced to little more than a cubicle in The University College Hospital; a black and white photograph of himself and herself in their prime that he asked me to bring in, his only possession. It was one of those shots taken of thousands of couples as they made their way down Patrick's Street, maybe to the Savoy Cinema or to a *John B Keane* play at The Opera House; in it my mother smiling in a tailored coat looking directly at the camera, leather-gloved and linking him; wearing a belted Macintosh, tie immaculately knotted, dapper, head tilted and looking at her proudly. The picture had stood on the sideboard and then many places thereafter, a constant over the years, moving from that starting point to the fireplace and the TV cabinet. Now it had reached its' final resting place, sharing space with a beaker and a *Lucozade* bottle. Leaving the hospital after he passed, they gave me a black bag.

"Your father's personal effects."

In truth nothing; a couple of faded pairs of pyjamas, slippers and a wash bag I had given him for the stay.

"You can keep that when you get out," I had reassured him, but he had looked at me resignedly, our eyes meeting, nothing more to say. At home, I sat with the clothes at my feet. Sometime after midnight, I dozed off, the clothes where they lay and the photograph on my lap.

Both Michael and my mother had been laid out in the house, and towards the end he had made it clear that he didn't want his any other way. He had no truck with fancy funeral homes.

"Too American," he spat out.

"Cold impersonal places. Don't bring me to one of those. Wasn't the house grand for your mother and the boy that time."

Not saying Michael's name, but I did what I always did-the right thing.

The neighbours?

They gave him a proper send-off-*a wake,* they called it in the papers. The hypocrisy of it was not lost on me, people who wouldn't give him the time of day alive pulling out all the stops. They couldn't have done enough, and I played along; just to be *sociable,* it was written. I didn't want to offend, and who would begrudge me. It was the end of an era.

A bad choice.

By the day of the burial, I was wiped out and by midnight there was no one left in the house, but a small group sitting around talking; the last of the stragglers, these so-called friends of the father, people I tolerated.

They were talking about shite mostly, yarns from Fords, stories I had heard a thousand times before. It had been a long three days. Someone opened the whisky.

"One for the road."

A toast for the old man.

And another one.

At around two I said I'd drop the last few home, just over the road, so no taxi was needed and I felt fine.

On the return journey home, as the rain hammered down, it dawned on me that finally I was alone. I had spent the previous three days trying to keep a lid on everything, and I had nothing left to give. It was time for some music. I had earned that, something appropriate; something that would capture the moment, a new beginning, a need I could meet with a *Spotify* shuffle play.

I remember that the green banner was unresponsive.

Oops, something went wrong.

I tapped again.

Nothing.

And again, annoyance gripping me that the magic moment would be lost.

It happened so fast. I just didn't see him, and I couldn't react.

The invisible boy.

I ran, and the guards found me hiding in a ditch panicked, and I'm not proud of that. Hiding like a drowned rat, praying to Jesus like I never prayed before.

"Please don't let him be dead-please."

And this Michael lying on the road twenty yards from where I struck him.

Two guards pulled me free, and the younger one looked absolutely terrified, the bigger guard roaring in my face:

"Do you know what you've done ya bollix ya, and do you know what we'll have to do later? Tell that boy's family. Tell that poor lad's screaming hysterical mother…It's a good hiding you'd want."

I wanted to tell them that I knew exactly what that felt like, but the words wouldn't come out. Back on the road there was heat, rain and a smell of death. The young guard felt faint and as the paramedics offered their assistance I thought of my mother.

The guards called to the house every couple of days for the first few months, going through all the gory details, reliving all over again the father's last weekend. When the visits stopped, the papers started. They had a field day reporting that I had been drinking for three days straight, a lie:

5 pints…3 half ones…two shots

A session I would never forget.

I pleaded guilty to dangerous driving causing death and at the trial Michael's family told the judge they did not want a custodial sentence:

"We know he did not set out to kill our beautiful son that night. He made a horrible choice, and he has his own life sentence now."

His mother spoke solemnly, fighting back her tears, while I shifted uneasily and stared at the floor. She continued, occasionally weeping softly, to tell us about her angel, her beautiful son with his whole life ahead of him snuffed out in a puff of smoke.

Told us how Michael's presence had filled the house and now all that remained was an endless void. It could have been my mother's story, the one she hadn't shared with me. Finally, she addressed me directly, explaining how she had:

"Thought long and hard about it."

But would forgive me, and me unable to forgive myself.

"A magnanimous act of forgiveness," the judge called it, taking the statement into account and handing me down 190 hours of Community service. Ten hours for every year of the boy's life, the papers reported.

I decided I was not going to hide from it and that I was going to stay visible.

The ultimate challenge for the invisible boy.

So, I pop into The Tavern daily for a coffee and a free read; retracing my father's footsteps and occasionally pausing to wonder what the neighbours would have to say about that.

Dreamers

Christmas Week 1942

Michael Lynch had been working at *The Market Sweet Factory* for fifteen years. The factory and all it encompassed dominated his life, just as it dominated the cobbled streets where it stood on Cork's northside. Michael was a proud northsider, and he had dedicated his life to the place, so when James Daly had retired as manager after over fifty years of service to sweet toothed Corkonians, everyone who was anyone knew that Michael Lynch was the natural successor. Everyone except the management committee of *The Market*, as it was affectionately known locally, who having met at *The Imperial Hotel,* deemed that a change of direction was needed and appointed one Vincent Bernstein, recently arrived in Cork, as the man to lead the home of Hadji Beys Turkish Delight into a bright new future. Michael Lynch buried his disappointment.

"The Jew," he growled; the only concession to resentment on hearing the announcement, while his close friends rallied around him. For his part, Michael had decided that this was only a minor setback, and he resolved to keep his head down for the greater good. He felt it was the perfect opportunity to reset, take a step back, dedicate himself more to *the cause* and spend more time with Madge.

"She just needs more time to get used to the idea," he thought to himself as he strolled through the warren of streets that led to *The Market.* Everybody was feeling under pressure to complete the Belfast order before the 23rd and come new year things would settle down. He was sure of it. He thought of Madge again. It would work itself out.

Madge Sullivan felt as if a great weight had been lifted. The last few weeks had felt oppressive, workdays dragging, walking on eggshells. She had needed to say it, and now it was said. The future looked bright. Even the monotony of the work could not dampen her spirits today.

"The order has to be in Belfast by the 23rd," she said, mimicking Michael Lynch. "If Michael Lynch says that one more time!"

Betty Donovan laughed.

"I know, all those people up in Belfast with their tongues hanging out for Turkish Delight, and they are supposed to be defending the empire against Hitler!"

The two women were alone and working in tandem. Madge Sullivan, a petite girl in her mid-twenties packing the hexagonal shaped boxes with Turkish Delight from the trays while the older woman, Betty Donovan, placed these smaller boxes into large wooden crates for transportation. It was hard physical work, but both women were skilled practitioners. Betty was regularly described by those who knew her as "a fine-looking woman in her day", but her features betrayed a world weariness that masked a maturing attractiveness.

"I know Mr. Bernstein was saying times were good up North now, never had it so good in London either for that matter," Madge answered.

"Booming", Betty said, not breaking her work rhythm.

"Plenty of work there, he said."

"He never says much to me."

"Vincent?"

"So, it's Vincent now."

"Give over Betty."

Betty Donovan stopped briefly from the task at hand:

"I spot things," she said.

"There's nothing to see."

Now the older woman turned to her younger work colleague.

"Be careful Madge. It's a dangerous game you are playing," she said authoritatively.

"Did it ever cross your mind, though?" Madge asked.

"What?"

"A fresh start…London…New York even…to get away, a new beginning."

"No," Betty answered without hesitation.

"Not even a thought."

"No. My Jim wouldn't entertain that in any shape or form."

"I think about it every single day, morning, noon and night."

"Aren't we happy enough as we are," Betty shrugged dismissively.

"Speak for yourself. I have plans."

"And what about Michael? That man is heartbroken enough as it is already, and that's another thing I want to talk to you about."

Madge raised her hand.

"Betty, stop. I don't want to talk about it."

The two women recommenced working in silence before Madge spoke again: this time quietly but with conviction.

"I want more…to travel…to see the world. My mind's made up."

"And your father will have something to say about that!" Betty replied.

Dominic Sullivan had run *The Shandon Inn* ever since the passing of his own father, and his grandfather had run it before him. Selling beer and spirits was in his blood, but his wife had died young, leaving him with an only daughter Madge to raise, and now his thoughts were turning to the future and the passing on of responsibilities at the business. Madge knew her father had plans for her in the pub, and she had put in shifts there from early childhood, from cleaning tables, running errands to serving the handful of regulars their pints of stout. She had thought long and hard about how she could let her father down gently. He was sure to be disappointed, but it wasn't for her. She hadn't told him yet of the grand vision she had for herself. She had seen Betty's life unfold at close quarters across the factory floor, and she did not want that for herself; the age difference between herself and husband Jim coupled with moving in under the same roof as his mother. Her childless life; signed, sealed, and delivered. Madge wasn't desperate and wasn't going to settle for the first fella with a few pounds to spare, no matter what her father thought. Michael knew that now. She had made it clear. She had money saved, her own money, and they would be drawing down the *diddlies* later in the week with the Christmas bonus to follow.

"I hope it stays fine for you," Betty continued. "The only bonus we got last year was a box of Hadji Beys to take home for our troubles!"

Not that Madge needed any reminding of the previous year's festive period and especially of the annual trip to the Christmas Ceili at *The Gresham Rooms* where Betty had coaxed her into giving Frankie Barry, the factory floor *go-for*, one dance. She could still see herself battling to keep him at a respectable distance and still hear him telling her:

"Your hair smells lovely altogether."

Afterward the girls laughed at Frankie's expense, but Madge also remembered how Michael Lynch had not seen the funny side and had remained in foul humour throughout the rest of the night for:

"Giving that omadhaun notions," as he put it.

Frankie, for his part, knew he was the butt of the girls' jokes on the factory floor, but he accepted this and often played the role with relish. He knew that Madge was Michael's girl, knew that nothing got done for *the cause* without Jim Donovan's say so, but his own father had been one of the 1st Cork Brigade killed in an ambush by the Black and Tans in Patrick's Street back in 1920 an attack Betty's husband Jim had also been injured in. Frankie Barry felt that gave him a status the others didn't have, and he was prepared to bide his time before an opportunity arose to prove himself. This he would not let rest, and he was determined to keep knocking on that door. He was sure that eventually it would open. Change was in the air. He could sense it, and he was determined to be part of it when Jim did make that call.

Michael Lynch and Madge were alone. Betty had gone home to serve up lunch, as was her daily routine.

"It can't be easy on Betty rattling around that big house with Jim and the mother," Michael said.

"I didn't know you cared."

"There's no respect there."

"I thought you were a big fan of his," Madge replied.

"That's different, he makes things happen."

"Grow up Michael," she snapped.

"I'm not the only one whose head is full of shite," he answered.

"So, you keep telling me."

Michael Lynch was tired, and he could see their conversation going down an all too familiar road.

"Jesus Madge, can't we not say two civil words to each other? I said I was sorry," he pleaded.

"You did"

"And I meant it."

"You always mean it, but then it happens again."

"So, you are still odd with me."

"Ah, I'm going for a walk," Madge said, and she turned to take her coat from the coat stand. As she did, Michael approached her from behind and slipped his hands around her waist.

"Michael! What do you think you are doing? Stop it!" she exclaimed in fright.

"Remember when it was only me you would walk out with," he said, continuing to hold her.

"Stop it, Michael! The others will back," she said, attempting to break free, but Michael Lynch tightened his grip.

"I don't care," he said.

Madge continued to struggle to break free and in doing so, managed to turn and face Michael, but he was holding her wrists now.

"Well, I do-so I said stop it," she said, raising her voice. "Do you want to get the both of us fired?"

"I couldn't give a fiddlers about this fucking place. It's you I care about," he said, refusing to release his grip.

"I told you, Michael. I just don't share those feelings. Now let me go."

"Can I not get you to see some sense," he said.

"Let me go, I said!"

This time Michael Lynch did release her, and Madge rubbed her wrists vigorously as she moved away from him.

"You were hurting me," she said.

"Can we not give it another go?" he asked.

"It's not for me."

"Jesus Madge, amn't I after saying I'm sorry. What more do you want from me?"

"It doesn't work like that," she said, slowly putting on her coat.

"We could make it work, the two of us."

"Stop it, Michael."

"Your father wouldn't be against it."

"For Christ's sake Michael, if you must know there's someone else."

"Someone else?" he said, appearing momentarily dazed.

"I didn't want to have to tell you…hurt your feelings, but you just wouldn't let it go."

Michael Lynch's initial confusion at the revelation was now giving way to anger.

"Someone else…hurt my fucking feelings!"

And now it was Madge's turn to flounder.

"Someone different," she said weakly.

"And what does that mean?"

"It's over-between us-finished."

"You don't mean it."

"It just is, alright."

"You're not thinking straight, none of us are."

"Don't Michael."

"We are all beat stupid from this place," he said as Madge made to leave, but Michael advanced on her one more time:

"Come on, Madge, just a kiss and a cuddle for old times' sake."

"No!!"

Frankie Barry wasn't going to take no for an answer. He was determined to talk to Michael as soon as an opportunity presented itself. They were working in silence now, and the girls were not due in for another twenty minutes, but Michael was stacking the wooden crates at a rate that Frankie was having trouble keeping pace with.

"What's eating you this morning anyway?" he asked attempting to slow the work down.

"Did anyone ever tell you to keep your nose out of other people's business," Michael answered, not relenting from the task at hand.

"Jesus, I was only asking."

"Well don't."

The two men continued to work in silence.

"They should have never passed you over for that job Michael," Frankie said eventually, attempting to catch breath.

"Well, they did."

"And I heard a lot of people saying it."

"Talk is cheap."

"Not fair at all."

"Don't you worry about me."

"Passing over one of their own."

"I said I'll be fine," Michael said, this time stopping briefly.

"And for a Jew. Shur everyone knows you'd run this place blindfolded," Frankie answered.

"'Tis a pity someone wouldn't throw a blindfold on you some night."

"Me?"

"Yes, you and run you up to Glanmire woods for a little spin."

"That's one thing Jim will never have to arrange," Frankie said firmly.

"I hope not," Michael said.

"I'm no rat for *the shades*. They'd never break me. I'd do time first."

"That's good to hear," Michael replied, and he began to work again.

"And was I mentioned?"

"When?"

"Last night."

"Maybe."

"I want to help *the cause.*"

Michael stopped again, and this time leaned across the crates to face Frankie.

"But can you be trusted, when the heat is on."

"One hundred percent," Frankie answered.

"You will have to prove yourself first. Something low-key."

"Just say the word. I won't be found wanting."

"No more talk here. There's work to be done," Michael said.

"I want to prove myself."

"Patience man-patience."

"Will you say it to Jim?"

Michael slammed one of the crates to the floor, almost spilling out the neatly packed boxes.

"What did I just say…not here…there's lads been lifted left right and centre over loose talk? Do you want me to get Jim to arrange that trip to Glanmire after all?". There was an edge to Michael's voice now.

"It's just I'm ready."

"Well, keep your head down so. Now where the bloody hell have those girls got to!"

Betty was late, and Madge scanned the quays anxiously for any sign of her whereabouts. The two women met every morning religiously at St Vincent's bridge to complete the short walk to *The Market.* They would spend this opportunity chatting freely, a luxury that was frowned upon on the factory floor by both Michael Lynch and James Daly before that. However, times were changing at *The Market* and Vincent Bernstein had come in with fresh ideas that included supplying a gramophone player on the factory floor; believing that this acquisition would be good for both workers' morale and productivity. Michael had scoffed at the idea, seeing it as nothing but a softening of *The Market's* traditional values. The girls, on the other hand, quite enjoyed the occasional hum along to Frank Sinatra's *I Wonder Who's Kissing Her Now* as they worked, the sole phonograph record in *The Market* collection.

This morning there would be no time for idle chat and Madge watched nervously as the last of the distillery workers hurried in through the gates of *Wyse's.* This hustle and bustle of the last-minute stragglers served to remind her that both herself and Betty should be doing likewise at their own workplace. The quays became quiet again and as the smell of hops slowly began to pervade the air, Betty finally came into view. She was walking slowly and seemed in no apparent hurry to make up for lost time.

"Jesus Betty! What kept you? Of all the weeks!!" Madge said, admonishing her friend.

"I fell," Betty said, pointing to the left side of her face. Her cheekbone was grazed, and she was sporting a fresh cut at the corner of her eyebrow and left eye. The wound was still open and looked angry. Madge was taken aback.

"Jesus, Mary and Joseph, what are you after doing to yourself?"

"I fell…this morning…bringing the clothes out to the line…too busy rushing about, that's all."

"Here, let me take a look," Madge said, examining Betty's face and acceding to her own request before Betty could reply.

"I'm fine…seriously…I'm just sorry I'm late, that's all."

Madge probed the cuts and grazes gently.

"You don't need to be apologising to me. Are you sure you are, ok?"

"I'm grand really, I am. I was just coming up the yard with the basket and tripped at the gate. You know that old gate of ours, Madge," Betty said, wincing occasionally at Madge's touch. Madge completed her examination:

"'Tis nasty enough."

"I said I'll be fine," Betty said.

"And what did Jim say?" Madge asked.

"Jim's cure for everything is a cup of tea. Now come on, we are late enough as it is already," Betty said as the two women began walking together in silence into a December greyness that was folding over the northside of the city.

"I don't know Betty. I think you should take yourself off to the *North Infirmary*," Madge said as the sights and sounds of the quays began to fade into the distance.

"I'm fine, I said…a few scratches," Betty answered.

"And that's all Jim had to say for himself-a cup of tea."

"Let it go, Madge."

"I can't."

"Please."

Both women stopped walking in unison, and it was Madge who spoke first.

"You can talk to me, Betty, if you want."

"There's nothing to talk about."

"But if there was…anything…You shouldn't have to put up with it. That's all I'm saying."

Betty took a breath.

"I drew him out," she said, patting the wound on her cheek. Both women were facing each other now.

"He's not entitled," Madge said softly.

"He gets short sometimes. He doesn't mean anything by it. He's not a bad man."

"So, you say," Madge answered, and the two women hugged each other spontaneously; a brief show of connection before continuing the final leg of their walk to work.

"Don't worry," Madge reassured Betty: "I'll straighten it with Mr. Bernstein."

Life was good for Vincent Bernstein; only six months in Cork and he was already making a life for himself, doing what his family hadn't thought possible. He knew they wouldn't share in his contentment at his good fortune, but he believed that they would in time come to an acceptance of the life he had chosen for himself. That was for another day, and now he looked out over the factory floor from the top of the stairs that led to his small, cramped office.

He watched as Michael Lynch and Frankie Barry loaded the wooden crates for the Belfast order. Michael looked sullen, and Vincent hoped it wasn't a portent for unrest. Managing Michael's disappointment at being passed over for manager hadn't been easy for Vincent, but he felt he had done a reasonable job of keeping Michael on side and thus ensuring a smooth transition of authority at *The Market.* The others were led and said by Michael, and Vincent was quite proud of how he had gone about resolving that conundrum.

The girls were also at their benches now working diligently. Madge had come to him to explain their lateness and he had made a public show of annoyance for the others to witness. They couldn't know, not yet, that a chance meeting with Madge down *The Coal Quay* had ignited a spark that had taken them both equally by surprise and had now blossomed into a fully-fledged passionate clandestine romance.

Vincent walked into his office and, sitting at his desk, read the letter from his father once more. On finishing it he folded it neatly and placed it in his jacket pocket. He thought of Madge. They needed to talk.

Madge had been expectant with excitement ever since Vincent had suggested this late-night meeting at *The Market,* so once he had let them inside, she could not contain herself anymore.

"Can I interest you?" she said, grabbing him playfully as he attempted to close the door behind them.

"For God's sake, Madge, cut it out," he said, attempting to fend her off and get the door closed as quickly as possible.

"I can't help it. I'm weak for you," she continued, but Vincent was determined to keep her at bay.

"Please, someone will see us from the street," he pleaded with her, but she was enjoying his discomfort.

"I don't care if the whole of Cork knows," she said as she began waving and calling out loud for the attention of anyone who might have been passing.

"You-who!! Over here."

Finally, Vincent did get the door closed.

"Come away, Madge, and stop your fooling around."

"Shur isn't that why you brought me up here in the first place, for a bit of fooling around," she laughed and pulled Vincent closer to kiss him.

"Shh," he said. "Now let me show you what I've brought you," he continued.

"Oh yes, surprise me. What?" she answered as he led her by the hand to the open space in the centre of the factory floor.

"Eyes closed, ok," he said as Madge played along willingly. Quickly, Vincent removed a lantern, rug and a bottle of wine from the bag he was carrying and set them down skillfully on the floor.

"No peeping," he said, lighting the lantern. "Now you can look."

"Well, well, aren't you the dark horse," Madge said on opening her eyes and they both sat on the rug where Madge took up the bottle of wine in her hand.

"And my God, where did you get this from?"

"From the pub," Vincent answered. "And that's not all," he added, before taking a corkscrew from his pocket and waving it triumphantly in the air.

"Your father charged me the control price and not a shilling more."

"He must have been delighted. He has no sale for it."

"He runs a fine business, so he does…now glasses!" Vincent said, standing up quickly and ascending the stairs to the office.

"Don't move," he said as Madge set the bottle down. She watched Vincent go into the office before getting up off the rug herself, taking a chair and crossing to the closed door with it. There she stood up on the chair.

"Madge! What are you doing?" Vincent asked as he alighted the stairs with two mugs in his hand.

"I brought a little surprise myself," she said, taking a sprig of red berried holly from her pocket and placing it above the door frame.

"For luck. I get it every year for here and the pub. Make a wish now. Go on. You can't tell me, though."

"I've been thinking about that," Vincent said, returning to the rug.

"Shh…let me make mine," Madge answered before stepping down off the chair to join him. The sound of the cork popping was like the opening of the gate to an illicit garden for two of them. And Vincent liberally filled both mugs.

"Right, spit it out," Madge said.

"I thought you said I couldn't," Vincent replied, handing Madge a mug.

"Ah, take no notice of me," she answered, the smell of the wine adding to her sense of giddiness. "Cheers," she added exuberantly, and they clinked their mugs together.

"This place is going to need all the luck it can get, but I think we will get by and turn the corner in the new year," Vincent said as they enjoyed their first tastes of the wine and soon Madge was feeling somewhat light-headed from the mix of racing adrenaline and the alcohol.

"You must miss your family, especially at Christmas," she said.

"No, not at all. Cork is my home now," Vincent replied, taking the opportunity to top up both mugs.

"My father felt that my coming to Cork was just a notion and something that I would get out of my system in a few weeks. I suppose it was at first, but then I got this job, and before you know it…"

"You fell for me," Madge said before kissing him again.

"I feel I belong."

"It will be brilliant though when we do go over to London. No more skulking around like this, worrying who might see us," she said.

"You haven't told your father."

"Not yet, but I'm going to, over the Christmas."

"You really know what you want, don't you, Madge."

"Of course. I want to get away and live my own life."

"If only it was that straightforward," Vincent said.

"It will be. And have you told your parents about me?"

"My father would say it's a "passing phase" and my mother would say nothing. They want me to be like them, I suppose, but that's not for me. I want to make my own home, my own life also." They were lying on the rug now, and Madge had her head placed on Vincent's lap.

"I can't wait," she said.

"It has to be kept quiet for now."

"It won't be for much longer, though."

"And why not?"

"Betty knows."

"Has she said something?"

"She sees things."

"Shit."

Madge could sense the alarm in Vincent's voice and turned to face him.

"What do we care who knows."

"It's complicated," he answered, moving the fringe from her eyes before kissing her again, this time their tongues probing one another sensitively.

"I know what we can do," Madge said, her face coming alight with anticipation. "Go to *The Gresham Rooms* together this week, and you can dance with me all night, sweep me off my feet. Will we do it, Vincent? The two of us. Imagine the look on their faces!"

"Do you think it's wise, rubbing people's noses in it," Vincent replied, but Madge was not listening anymore and had already jumped to her feet, pulling Vincent up with her.

"Dance me here, then!" she said, her strength taking Vincent by surprise.

"Steady now, Madge…steady," Vincent said, trying to resist, but Madge was free from all inhibitions now and began leading him erratically across the factory floor. Madge was laughing freely and before long Vincent was allowing himself to be guided on this dervish waltz before they both spun out of control and sent the gramophone player crashing to the ground. There was a moment of silence before Madge began to laugh uncontrollably, an unrestrained laugh that brought Vincent to his senses.

"Jesus Madge…shh," he said, before a wild knocking at the door and a familiar voice brought further sobriety to them both.

"Hey! What's going on in there? Open this door!!"

They both held their breath and listened as the door was rattled once more, but there was no mistaking. It was Frankie Barry.

Betty Donovan had enough. All morning, the rhythm of the work had hung like a millstone over the factory floor.

"And is that all he said…that he thought the place was being robbed," she asked, but Madge remained engrossed in her work.

"Madge! Frankie Barry is that all he said?" she asked again, determined to get to the bottom of it.

This time Madge did answer.

"Ah…I don't give a damn about what he says or the sky over him," she answered.

"And the mouth on him. The whole of the northside will know it by now," Betty replied.

"And do you think I care?"

"And has Michael said anything?"

"No…and have you anything better to be doing? Can't you see I'm busy!" Madge shot back angrily, and the two women recommenced the work in silence.

"It can't be easy for Michael either," Betty said eventually.

"And what's he got to do with the price of bacon!" Madge said, reacting angrily.

"You know right well what."

"He will just have to live with it."

"And your father?"

"Leave him to me."

Routine descended once more on the two women, but Betty's inquisitiveness had opened a door, and Madge eventually grasped the opportunity to walk through it.

"Vincent has asked me to leave with him."

"Has he now?"

Yes, to London."

"Ah London…shur that settles it."

"We won't leave this place in the lurch. We will see the order through," Madge said.

"That's big of ye."

"Can you not just be happy for me?"

"I am a proper bitch aren't I! Telling you what you should be doing with your life, and I can't sort my own," Betty said.

"It's never too late."

"My race is run. Jesus, look at the state of me!" There was an emotion in Betty's voice now that Madge had never heard before.

"And did you ever love him?"

At first, it appeared to Madge that Betty hadn't heard her at all. She appeared transfixed, in a place Madge could never share.

"Love? T'was company and security I was after. That's the way I saw it. The love would come later. That's the choice I made," Betty said, composing herself once more.

"It's a terrible way to live," Madge answered.

"For me, it's the only way. I have some good weeks…months. They make up for the bad days," Betty continued strongly, with no hint of emotion.

"I want good years," Madge said, looking directly at her friend.

"Wishing, hoping and dreaming will only get you so far…just…just take it steady. People could get hurt."

"I'll do that for you, Betty, if you do one thing for me," Madge answered.

"If I can."

Madge stood up from her workstation and crossed to stand where Betty was seated. She leaned in enthusiastically, their faces almost touching.

"Come along with us to *The Gresham Rooms* on Wednesday night," she said.

"Dancing!" Betty laughed, throwing her head back in amusement.

"And what harm is in that, a couple of hours," Madge said encouragingly.

"I can't. Jim is expecting a caller, an important one. He likes me to stay for callers. He'll need me," Betty said, her expression becoming withdrawn once more.

Madge slapped the workbench in frustration.

"Can't his blasted mother look after him for once!"

"You don't understand. Shur that's what started it," Betty said, pointing to her bruised face before laying out without a shred of emotion of how this "latest spat", as she described it, had unfolded and of how Jim had told her of his German friend who needed a safe house to stay in for a few days and of how she had tried to put a stop to it, put her foot down, but this "new face" of hers was her "thanks for it".

"Jesus, Betty, you can't let him away with it," Madge said on hearing the explanation.

"And you must solemnly swear never to breathe a word to anyone. If he thought for one moment, I was telling you this kind of information."

Those consequences were clearly written in Betty's eyes and Madge felt totally helpless in the face of this fear and desperation.

"But is there anything, anything at all I can do to help?"

"Yes, there is," Betty assured her firmly, "Let this conversation be the last of it."

"And Wednesday night, will you come?"

"Maybe."

※

Vincent Bernstein was uneasy. He could have kept Frankie Barry quiet with a few boxes of Hadji Beys, but the genie was out of the bottle now. He needed to sit down with Madge; sort their future out once and for all.

"Him finding out might be the best thing that ever happened," Madge said when they finally did get a moment alone.

"My settling here in Cork is the best thing that ever happened," he answered.

"And I want to be with you and leave with you. My mind is made up, so to hell with the begrudgers," Madge said as she attempted to hug him.

"You need to listen to me Madge. We need to talk-get things straight," he said, stopping her short.

"I just want us to start our life together," Madge continued.

"And we will," Vincent answered, taking her in his arms. "I love you, Madge," he said, holding her gently now. "It's just everything is happening so fast. People need to get used to the idea."

"It will be brilliant, Vincent-brilliant altogether," Madge said, hugging him exuberantly in return.

"Listen my love," Vincent said before taking the letter from his pocket. "This came from my father,"

"Yes, go on, tell me. Is there news?"

"He wants me back, in London."

"Brilliant. It's settled then. London, and I have so much to do, my father. I will tell him straight away tonight."

"Please Madge. I just want to get this right," Vincent said, taking her hands in his.

"Your hands. They're shaking!"

"They are, aren't they," he answered. "I have done this a thousand times in my mind, and you don't have to say anything straight away."

Madge was watching his face closely as he spoke now, and it betrayed a previously unseen vulnerability.

"What are you trying to say," she asked.

"I'm trying to explain."

"Explain what, you are not really making any sense."

Vincent took a breath. "…My…running away."

"I haven't the foggiest idea what you are on about, Vincent. Running away from what?"

"My father and his grand plan."

"What are you saying to me," Madge said, taking a step back.

"The study of medicine, Madge. that's what I'm on about, the good Doctor Bernstein's legacy to his only son, the family tradition."

"Medicine?" Madge answered, standing motionless.

"Yes Madge, but I don't want it and I won't do it," He was brandishing the letter now. "And now the game is up. He wants me back," Vincent continued before opening the letter to read from it:

"It's time to face up to your responsibilities, your duty to serve medicine and end this outrageous charade. Time to return home immediately and resume your studies before bringing further ignominy on the Bernstein family name…"

"Show me that!" Madge said, snatching the letter from his hands to read it for herself.

"A student! What else haven't you told me? Do you even love me or is that all talk too!"

"No listen. I wanted to tell you sooner, but…"

"You thought I wouldn't want to stay with you because you're a student."

"No, it's not like that at all."

"Of course, I will. I can get a job. There's plenty of opportunities for good, hard working girls in London. We can work this out together."

"It's not what I want for us," he said, taking the letter back from Madge.

"But your father is right, Vincent," she answered.

"I was thinking that the two of us could make a go of it here," he said, folding the neatly and putting it back in his pocket.

"Here?"

"Yes."

"Are you joking me?"

"That we could even make a go of the pub."

"That place."

"Yes…together."

"You're actually serious."

"Totally," Vincent said, stepping forward towards Madge, but now it was her stopping him short.

"And London?"

"We don't need that."

"Jesus, listen to yourself. We can't stay here, not now," Madge said as panic gripped her.

"We could make a decent life together."

"You haven't even told your family about me. Have you?"

"I don't need to. I know them, Madge. They'd never allow it."

"Jesus, I want a life!"

"And so do I."

"Cleaning out ashtrays and smelling of stale beer is it."

"If that's what it takes to make a future. What do you say?" he asked.

"We need to leave, Vincent. We will never be accepted here."

"We can make it work," he said, moving once again to embrace her.

"I need to think," Madge said, shrugging him off forcefully.

"We love each other, Madge. Isn't that enough?"

"Love! You're living in dreamland!!"

Madge Sullivan's mind was racing. The future she had mapped out for herself so precisely was slipping agonisingly through her fingers. She couldn't stomach dancing, not now, not to-night, but Betty had agreed to meet her for an hour at *The Gresham Rooms* and Madge was sure that Betty would know how to proceed and what needed to be done to make Vincent see sense. Madge was running late, but if she cut through *The Rock Steps,* she could make up the lost time…

…Michael Lynch couldn't explain why he hadn't simply called out to Madge when he saw her making her way through Blackpool but chose to follow her instead. She seemed agitated as she turned down *The Rock Steps.* All he wanted was somewhere quiet to iron things out.

"Jesus, Michael, you put the fear of God in me coming up behind me like that. My nerves!"

"We need to talk, Madge."

"Look Michael, we had a few nights on the town…a laugh and a giggle," she said, attempting to pass him, but he was facing her now and blocking her route.

"And that's it."

"Yes."

"Fun and games."

"And you wouldn't leave it that," Madge continued, standing her ground now.

"Jesus Madge. I'm crazy for you. There I've said it. Is that what you want to hear?"

"No, Michael. Did I ever once mention that?" she answered.

"Hear me out."

"Drop it, Michael."

"I won't drop it: we have to talk."

"Do we?"

"Properly."

"Ah, I'm in no mood for talking, so let's just leave it before one of us says something we will regret," she said.

"The Jew dumped you, so now you are taking it out on me," Michael Lynch replied with anger now consuming his face.

"Who told you that?" Madge laughed dismissively.

"I find things out."

"Gossip," Madge answered and once again attempted to pass Michael on the steps, but this time he blocked her path more forcefully:

"Who cares who said it."

"Because it's not true," she answered, taking a step backwards.

"Face it, Madge, you made a proper eejit of yourself."

"You don't know what you are talking about."

"I know you were supposed to be off to London, and he let you down and that you never saw it coming, thought the sun, moon, and stars shone out of his arse and all the time he was leading you up the garden path."

Madge didn't flinch. She didn't care who knew what anymore, and at that moment she only felt a strange sense of pity for Michael; a pity she could understand only too well:

"Will you give over before you make a total fool of yourself. You have got the complete wrong end of the stick," she said.

"Ah Christ Madge, I don't care about the ins and outs of it. I forgive you."

"You forgive me…for what?" Madge said, flinching with indignation.

"Your head was turned."

"If you must know, Vincent wants the two of us to make a go of the pub."

"Your fathers place."

"Yes, together, the both of us."

"Here…in this city." There was incredulity written all over Michael Lynch's face.

"You heard me."

Michael Lynch took two steps back as if he needed the space to process what he was hearing, what was being laid out before him by the girl he loved, so coldly and so calmly, before the cold air seemed to snap him back to the reality of what he was facing.

"That is not going to happen, girl," he said, advancing on her aggressively.

"Just call it quits boy," Madge answered dismissively as he grabbed her by the shoulder and thrust her forcefully towards himself:

"Rubbing my nose in it like that. If only I didn't love you so much."

"Look, Michael, I never loved you!" Madge screamed at him, stumbling backwards as she attempted to break free.

"You and the fucking Jew! I can't let that happen Madge!!

"This bastard left her for dead, but there will be no stone left unturned," Vincent Bernstein explained solemnly, but Michael Lynch knew that already. He hadn't slept, his mind tearing itself into two.

"If only he hadn't loved Madge so much."

What once would have been music to his ears was merely a white noise to him now. Vincent Bernstein was thinking of "taking a step back" and going to recommend Michael as the one to step up, over a lunch at *The Imperial* hastily arranged for later that day.

"This place is in your blood Michael, and you drove the Belfast order on this week. You could run this place blindfolded."

The pace of change only added to Michael's sense of despair. He listened numbly as Vincent Bernstein shared that he needed to return to London; "to sort out the future."

By mid-morning it was like the whole city was in a grip of police raids, truths and half-truths.

"The poor girl will never be the same."

"She's a fighter."

The usual suspects were being rounded up, Frankie Barry, released without charge, and Jim Donovan, the safe house not so safe anymore.

"He will get a few months again in *The Curragh* for sure." Betty, his long-suffering wife, remained stoic. "But you know it might be the chance I need to make a small trip myself. I have a cousin in Birmingham…let Jim and the mother fend for themselves for a change… put myself first."

"If only I didn't feel so fucking tired," Michael Lynch thought to himself as he sat alone on the factory floor.

"Frankie Barry would get his chance for sure now-to be a leader."

But that was for another day. Michael was due down to the station at four to make his own "routine statement" and provide details as to his own "whereabouts" for the "time in question.", but he also knew that couldn't wait and that he needed to do the right thing for Madge. He stood up and crossed to the coat stand, where he put on his coat slowly and methodically. He then crossed the factory floor for what he knew was the last time and as he closed *The Market* door finally behind him, a sprig of red berried holly fell to the floor.

A Family Affair

People always said I was a right "stubborn bastard", and maybe that's what it came down to in the end. You see, in my time you lived hard, played hard, second was first loser and there was never any problem that couldn't be solved by a kick in the bollocks. I'm sure that's why Sheila fell for me in the first place.

The first time I saw him…I'll always remember that; not an arse in his trousers and a big red raw spot on the side of his nose. There was a bunch of fellas that always hung around "The Arc" and to be honest, I don't know what I saw in him, took pity on him most of all. Christ, I wanted to take him home and give him a good wash and a good feed. Three weeks later, we were an item, and I was pregnant on my seventeenth birthday.

I had to do the decent thing. I wouldn't abandon any girl in trouble of that nature. Like my father said at the time: "wouldn't it make a man of me."

My father? Took it well enough. Looked me straight in the eye and said, "I'll castrate the weedy fucker!"

I don't think her auld fella was switched on to the idea.

We were married in May 1962. You couldn't call it a wedding as such. My parents were there, Jack's father and me six months gone with Maurice. The doctors came the night he was born and told me it was touch and go, a very difficult delivery. I had worked out that much for myself.

I spent the night having a few pints with the lads. I mean, I was a real man now and let's face it, it's not exactly a spectator sport. Anyway, we were all well jarred when someone decided I should put a call through. A snotty-nosed young one answered, wanting to know who I was and how I was connected to the mother. I asked to speak to the matron, and she said "speaking" putting on a right tone mind you. I couldn't let her get away with that and told her how it was me and others like me that were keeping her in her bloody job. She went on to give me a lecture about not facing up to my responsibilities for my troubles. I knew all that, knew it was time to get my arse in gear. I had a son to rear now. My round.

I spent a lonely night thinking about my newborn child and what kind of future I could offer him. We would call him Maurice, after my own father. That would take the sting out of it for him. There would be no arguments about that.

Of course, she was intent on making a Cissy out of the boy and things were moving fast, too fucking fast. One minute I was getting a quick rub and a squeeze at the front gate and the next thing I knew I had a wife and child to look after. I needed to start putting some serious money on the table, and fast. I wasn't going to let it be said that I couldn't provide for my own family, so I got a job driving for a haulage company down *The Marina*, the Dublin, Belfast routes, that kind of thing and out on the road you were your own boss. Life always looked better from the cab, clearer, less complicated. I knew that the long hours and the night runs would be worth it in the finish. Maybe someday Maurice would have a place in college, or who was to say a younger sister wouldn't come along and pioneer advances in medical science. Sheila would thank me for it later.

When Jack arrived home in one of his moods, he was best humoured. He had a savage temper on him, and, of course, that would set the child off.

That fucking young fella.

Nobody ever spoke about it, said anything, not in so many words, but I knew I was different. Children have a sense for stuff like that. There were little things like how everyone in my class wanted to be George Best and Steve Heighway was my man. I remember when *The Sunday World* started first, there was a pull-out cartoon section for the kiddies and a colour poster of the latest pin-up or whoever. They would publish a week in advance who was coming up next. The Sunday, I read it was Steve Heighway, I was well-made up. I prayed that someday I would grow up to be like him. I really wanted to be Muhammad Ali, but since most of the guys in my class could beat the shite out of me, I knew that no amount of praying could fix that. They'd often row about that at night when he'd come in late. I'd hear them at it.

"Jesus Christ, you are going to destroy that young fella. He'll have to fight his corner. I'm telling you. You'll make a laughingstock of the boy."

Saturdays were different. On Saturday nights, she'd let me stay up. It was fucking brilliant. You'd be sitting there waiting, and you'd have a knot of excitement in your stomach because you didn't know what he'd appear with. One time I remember I was saving the coins that were a giveaway with Shell petrol. Each coin had an imprint of a different make of car on it, and there was a special collector's board you could slot them into. Anyway, I was four shy of completing the set and this Saturday he comes in and takes the four coins I needed from his pocket. The three of us sat on the floor and filled in the card, him with a big grin on his face and my mother smiling.

Things were cool between us. Jack seemed to be working all hours of the clock. Don't get me wrong, it's not that I didn't appreciate the effort. It's just, I wanted something more, more romance. I was still a young woman, after all.

I was breaking my balls and I still couldn't please her.

The first night he hit me, I wanted to lay down and die. I remember it as if it was only yesterday. A memory like that stays with you forever. It was out of the blue. He had been gone for well over a day, and he arrived home one evening with a head on him. He grunted at me for five or ten minutes while he picked at his supper, and then I tried to make some small talk.

"Maurice is starting in the school choir tomorrow."

"He is in his shit."

The crack was like a gunshot going off in my head, and then a numbness followed by a sick feeling in the pit of my stomach. All I wanted to do was pass out, but I hung in there. I got better at it over the years. The odd Saturday night he'd come in with a smell of drink off him, as high as a kite and making a right fuss out of Maurice, laughing, joking and horse playing with him in the front room. I could relax then. As a family, it was as much as we ever saw of him.

I had a big red *Leyland* and when I wasn't tinkering around with her to keep her on the road, I spent the rest of my time at the handball. To be honest, it was a big weakness of mine—and I mean big. You see, at that time there was a ball alley on the main Dublin route adjacent to a restaurant called *Maggie's* where all the truckers stopped. *Maggie's* was a twenty-four- hour gaff, the kind of place you would get the breakfast menu at any hour of the day or night. The lunch menu was steak, full stop. They had other stuff on the board, but all they ever had was steak, and it was always cremated with lashings of mushrooms and onions. They never even bothered to ask how you liked it done. The first day I went in I saw thirty-five other lads all eating steak and I fell in love with the place straight away. Once the grub was finished, a gang of us would make our way across to the ball alley and give it a right good lash there. We'd always have a few pounds riding on it, just to spice things up a bit.

I saw my first naked woman in that alley. One of the men had just done a run through England to

France, and all the others were buzzing around him like bees around the honey pot. Now I knew what was going on, I wasn't that stupid, but when I tried to get a better look into the magazine he was holding, my auld fella gave me a right good clip around the ear. She was a beautiful black girl with incredible breasts, so incredible that I needed another clip from my father to shift me. I knew Muhammad Ali would have no problem getting a girl like that. The father had begun taking me riding in the cab of his big old *Leyland* with him over the summer months. All human life was there in that ball alley and when it came to the handball he was tops. He, being my father benefitted me into the bargain. There were spin-offs. The younger truckers would nod in your direction, while the old geezers often bought me cokes. I was ten years old, and it was cool.

Jack had gotten a notion into his head that Maurice needed to learn more from life than just what school could offer.

I was making a bit of a name for myself at handball and soon we were gambling more than loose change on the games. The way I figured it, by the time management and herself had a cut of the money I was earning, I had nothing left for myself, so what harm if I could generate some extra cash from the sporting skills God gave me. The plan was that the sooner I could branch out and put a truck of my own on the road, the better. I looked on every game won in that ball alley as an investment in Maurice's future.

He took me to Dublin on the train to buy his new truck. I had my heart set on a *Leyland,* and there was a beautiful blue one there gleaming in the yard.

But a couple of big money games had gone against me, and I couldn't get that kind of cash together, so in the end I had to settle for an eight-year-old *Hino.*

A Hino.

It never brought me a day's luck.

Twas around that time that Jack got to think we should have another child. I don't know how he thought we could afford it. I was seeing less of him, if anything, and there seemed to be more bills by the minute.

That fucking truck! I thought a daughter would be nice…to complete the family.

This…obsession didn't bother me in the slightest. I felt a baby would give me something to do and although money was tight, I was sure I could make it work. At worst, a pregnancy would give me a respite from Jack, the nights he came in with a feed of drink on him. My due date was August 1st, 1972.

By July, the top of my head was about to explode. Money was tight. I had been undercut on a few contracts and my slump in form at the ball alley continued. However, I met this guy in a pub in Dublin one night, and he offered me a border run with a load of dodgy diesel, a one-off, to see how I got on. Only the same fella was having a bit of a cash flow problem at the time and all he could offer me in return were a couple of Hogan Stand tickets to see Ali in Croke Park.

Fly like a butterfly, sting like a bee.

Like I say, I was having one of those summers. She couldn't understand it, but I knew that if I could carry off this diesel job, it would be worth my while in the long run. Put other work my way.

The fight couldn't come quick enough for me.

The day of the fight, we left Cork around midday so that we could take our ease and arrive at Croke Park with time to spare. The plan was to stop at *Maggie's* at half one for a bite to eat and then on to Dublin for the fight. *Maggie's* was quiet and me and the young fella were just about to leave when these two traveller lads came in. They had been by before, and I had seen one of them throwing a few shapes in the ball alley.

Packie McDonagh.

As I was passing him out, he started up: "any of ye lads looking to play some handball. There isn't a man among ye who'll bate me." We had an hour to kill.

I remember feeling nauseous. At that age, your father is a superhero, Mr. Invincible, and you don't get to see him piss that down the toilet.

... So maybe I shouldn't have put the tickets on the line.

I was ten years old.

Twas only a Mickey Mouse bout anyway, exhibition stuff, a money-making racket.

I ended up sitting in the cab of the *Hino* outside a pub in Abbeyleix. He always had enough left for drink. He never lost everything. It was after twelve before he came out to me. I could smell the drink off him, and for the first time in my life I was afraid. Afraid of my own old man.

Packie fucking McDonagh.

Your life can turn upside down in two minutes and there is nothing you can do about it. I spent the night at home resting. The pregnancy was tough going the second time round, and I had picked up a summer cold I had trouble shaking. In fact, my doctor had advised me to take it easy and avoid agitation. It must have been three in the morning when they arrived back. At that stage, I was up to ninety wondering if they were turned up in a ditch somewhere, and then Maurice came running into the hall in a terrible state.

Making an awful racket…no call for it.

But I managed to calm him down and get him to bed.

And then she starts on me.

I might have said something, but I'm sure it wasn't much. I caught him with the back of my hand, bloodied his nose with my wedding ring, trying to protect myself. Jack drew more than blood and by the time the ambulance arrived I knew the baby was lost. At the hospital, I could tell the doctors knew. I could see it in their eyes. There were no more relations after that.

I never felt the same about the ball alley after that and began counting the days for school. When we stopped there now, all I could think about was that night. They still bought me cokes and let me read their magazines, but most days Packie McDonagh was there.

I threw all my efforts into trying to feel good about myself again, even got away to a dance in Fermoy one night, the parents looking after Maurice…they knew the score. One of those nights when Jack didn't make it home. A women's night out, but I wanted to feel that again, a few dances, nothing serious-not that night.

I tried to throw myself into the work and make it up to her, but everywhere I turned I was snookered. My border run was just starting to make some serious money, but *the troubles* put the kibosh on that completely. Suddenly, there were guys in balaclavas coming on the telly spouting that southern regs were legitimate targets. I mean, there was no way I was that fucking desperate for business. And then the oil crisis tore the complete arse out of the haulage game. Put the tin hat on it.

Finally, it got to the stage that I had to get a part-time job serving behind the bar in a place on Wellington Road. The economy might have been in a downward spiral, but people had plenty of money in their pockets for drink. Jack was living proof of that.

Before the oil crisis hit, I hardly knew what the word economy meant for fuck's sake and now to be out of work. There was nothing worse. Any self-respect a man had was being taken away from him. The only people who seemed to be making a go of it were the travellers. If it wasn't the scrap metal or carpets, it was televisions. Packie McDonagh was in the thick of it. He took Cork by storm with a consignment of 24- and 26- inch monstrosities, set up a base in a lay-by on the Dublin Road and sold them like they were going out of fashion. If you brought one back that didn't work, he just fucked it over the ditch and gave you a replacement. He was coining it. The story being put about was that they were bringing them in from the north out of factories that were being bombed by the I.R.A.

Imagine that. Bringing out lorry loads of tellies and bombs going off all round you.

The old man said he wouldn't take a present of one, not that I had much time to watch it anyway. By now, he spent most of his time mooching around the house, so I knuckled down to the Leaving Cert. I desperately wanted them to get on...needed it.

I'd be working Friday, Saturday and Sundays, so Thursday was the big girls' night out, and it felt good. One evening we didn't make it to the ballroom, and we stayed chatting with a gang of fellas we met in the pub. He told me how I reminded him of someone from the films, silly carry on, really, and I encouraged it. Later, Patrick walked me home. At our place, he touched me gently, not like how I remembered Jack's touch. This was warm, safe.

The *Hino* was on its last legs. There were a host of jobs to be done on her, small odds and ends, but when they start giving trouble at all. One day, I did go as far as *Maggie's* for a spin. There was a younger crowd around, sales reps and the like, no one I knew. They were making the restaurant smaller and putting in a coffee bar. You see, these lads had no time for steaks, no time for handball.

I could have done without the rows, the endless bickering. It did my head in. I mean, what kind of exam preparation was that? There seemed to be no end to it, especially after he sold the *Hino*.

Packie McDonagh gave me three hundred quid for it. There was an oil leak that got the better of me. He said he'd use it for parts.

"Patrick."

"Whore! I never looked at another fucking woman!"

This was an eight on the Richter scale.

I woke up the next morning and stopped blaming myself. I'd wait till the Leaving Cert results were out for Maurice's sake, but I was damned if I was going to end up in the river. I had thought about that once or twice in my darkest hours, but I wasn't going to let Jack off the hook like that.

August couldn't come quick enough for me. I just had to get away, or I felt they'd drag me down with them.

"Four honours and three passes."

Journalism in Rathmines.

"That's my boy!"

We were means tested and the old man being unemployed meant I was eligible for the grant.

Call it making my contribution to my son's education.

I threw myself into it hook, line and sinker. At first, I'd go home for the weekends, and you'd get the washing done and a decent meal. I felt…obliged, obliged to sit around and play the peacemaker.

Patrick and I were still an item. Jack knew it, but he would not dare lift a finger anymore. It was nothing I'd said or even done. It was more a state of mind. We both just knew. Those days were gone.

"Tramp!"

"I'd like you to leave, Jack."

"You will have to throw me out."

"Is that your last word on it?"

"Yes."

"Right so. I want you out."

I arrived home for Christmas, and he was gone. Finito. Got himself a bedsit on Patrick's Quay. I called down Christmas night and for a few hours on New Year's Day. We had *Bourbon Cream Biscuits* and tea.

"You're coping."

"No fear of me. And how is herself?"

"Fine."

Whenever I made it home, I'd call. Most times he was out. He could have been dead somewhere and we wouldn't have known it.

I left for Liverpool in October 86. I wanted to make a clean break. There was nothing happening for anyone my vintage at home. I called to tell her. My duty.

"I never fooled around. Not once."

"I never said you did. And have you a place to stay?"

"Don't you worry about me at all."

I was still seeing Patrick, but on my terms. I knew he would have married me if he wanted that, but I was happy the way I was. In truth, I couldn't do that to Jack. He had lost enough.

It gave me something to cling to. Everybody deserves that much.

And that came between me and Patrick in the end. He wanted a family, needed one, for completion, and I couldn't give him that. Patrick hid his disappointment at first, but I could sense it until we drifted apart because of it. There was no devastation on my part. Yes, I loved him, but I had made a new life for myself now and had been down that road before. I knew the pitfalls.

At first, I worked freelance, scavenging for jobs here and there until I landed a job with *The Longford Leader. New York Times* how are you! I even called the old man and he seemed genuinely pleased.

"And this is a proper job now?"

"Yes."

"A reporter."

"Small-town gossip. That sort of thing."

"You had a good grounding."

And then I met Maria at a disco in Longford one weekend. Well, it wasn't really a disco, just an excuse for the pub, where I drank, to stay open until two o'clock in the morning. Any time more than ten people ventured out on to the excuse for a dance floor, the DJ's records skipped all over the shop. I had caught Maria's eye during one of the breakdowns in proceedings, and within weeks it was serious. By Christmas, we were engaged and planning a summer wedding. I wanted him there, so I arranged to meet him at a bar in Liverpool.

"To be honest, mam doesn't think this is a good idea. Thinks it will be awkward for both of ye."

"You came anyway."

"How are you? You look…"

"Wrecked?"

"I was going to say thin."

"On the good days you are an Irish Paddy. On the bad days, an Irish prick."

"I'd like you to be there."

"We'll watch the game first…see what happens."

By half-time, the game was abandoned. We sat there watching in silence as Liverpool supporters ripped down the advertising hoardings to stretcher their dying friends across the pitch, watching as people clawed desperately for breath against the steel fencing. Some hours later, we walked numbly through the empty streets of a city in mourning to his lodgings. There, as we stood in the half-light of a streetlamp, he looked gaunt and ashen faced.

"You're not coming dad, are you…to the wedding?"

"No, I'm not, son."

That feeling you don't get too often in a lifetime. I had gotten it once before; on the night he lost those Ali tickets. It was one of those days, and I gave up on him after that. Got on with my new beginning.

I wasn't surprised and thought it was for the best in the long run. Maurice needed to be making his own life now, a new life, and I became a proud Grandmother to Stephen in January 96.

Now that I was a father myself, it brought it home to me, so we booked a couple of nights in *The Moat Hotel,* in Liverpool city centre. I wanted him to meet them both, but he didn't feel there was anything to be gained by it. Now he was staying in the Y.M.C.A and looked wrecked.

"Do you remember the Shell coins, Dad?"

"I can't say I do. Why do you ask?"

"It's just the greatest night of your life is when you least expect it, and then it's gone. Are you sure you

won't change your mind? We can be over there in five minutes."

"I am. Tell your mother I was asking for her."

"Of course."

"Do you ever see that tinker anymore?"

"Traveller, dad."

"Yeah, that tinker who was after your mother."

"He's well gone."

"I knew it wouldn't last."

Back at the hotel, Maria and I booked a babysitter and stayed up drinking in the residents' lounge. As the night dragged on, a group gathered around the TV to watch a trembling Muhammad Ali open the Olympic Games. In an alcoholic haze, I longed for the grace, poise and beauty of my youth. Driving back from the ferry, my curiosity got the better of me. We pulled off the motorway and, leaving the bypass behind, went in search of my father's old stomping ground. I eventually found it. Where *Maggie's* once stood proudly was now a littered wasteland. At the entrance the council boulders to prevent anyone setting up camp there, not that anyone would be interested in such a remote spot these days, even if they had tellies to sell. The ball alley was overgrown and smaller than I had imagined. As we stood there amidst the echoes of those distant days, a cold chill came over us. "This place gives me the creeps," Maria said as Stephen started to cry. I knew at that moment this was my family now. We returned to the car and headed for McDonald's.

While Maintaining Social Distancing

Ireland
Holy Thursday 2020

Eamon stood in the unkempt garden, of his end of terrace home, with his front door slightly ajar. In truth, both had seen better days; the door having taken on a mottled appearance over the years to reveal the assortment of previous colours that had adorned it and the garden now pock marked with a mixture of bald patches and burnt grass. Several plant pots lay upturned, adding to the aura of decay, while the early morning dew cloaked the bristles of an idle sweeping brush. Eamon knew there were jobs to be done, work he had put on the long finger, but his previous house pride was becoming ever increasingly trumped by his own seventy-years-a- growing.

He scanned the footpaths and road that led to his cul-de-sac. She was late. Every morning since lockdown, like clockwork at eight thirty, moving quickly:

Pit pat…Pit pat.

Rubber on footpath, the girl passed before turning sharply at the wall and off again.

The loneliness of the long-distance runner.

It was her luminous runners he had spotted that first morning from his galley kitchen window; hi-vis yellow. It brought him back to his time at the school, boots black, runners white and then the Adidas boot with the white sole, another item of footwear that caught his eye.

What he had noticed first.

Today he had taken the liberty of stepping into his tiny garden. He glanced at his watch and wondered what was keeping her. Maybe she had met someone? Had a late night? A few drinks? Or maybe simply a change of route, a snap decision, fate?

Pit pat…Pit pat.

Luminous runners.

The girl moved effortlessly along the footpath, her hair meandering behind her, an auburn contrail. Approaching the wall, she adjusted her stride, slowed and turned in one graceful movement. As she did, Eamon stepped forward.

"I was just thinking you were late," he said, resting both arms across his garden gate and causing her to break momentum mid-stride.

"I thought I missed you this morning," Eamon continued, the girl now standing opposite him on the footpath.

"Sorry?" she replied as she removed two small white earphones.

"I was just saying you seem a bit late this morning."

"I am…I had to make a stop."

"Ah, don't take any notice of me," Eamon shrugged. "I'm just thinking out loud."

"I left early to avoid the checkpoints," the girl answered.

"You broke the law."

"I won't tell if you don't. It will be our little secret."

"They accused me of the same."

"And?"

"Nothing came of it."

"Good," the girl replied as she stepped closer to the gate. Eamon could now see the slight strain in her face that comes with exercise and the beads of perspiration that had formed on her blue running singlet where the straps of a neat backpack lay.

"Like I say, I was just thinking you were late, that's all, wondering were you ok and not in a spot of bother."

The girl smiled. "That's so sweet. I'm glad I have someone to look out for me. I need that sometimes and have you someone to keep an eye on you?" she asked.

"Not anymore…but one time twenty-four seven."

"That must be difficult for you so," she said, her demeanour filling with concern.

"I'm used to it."

"If you need anything, I could help," she said.

"I don't want to cause any trouble," Eamon said and made a swatting gesture with his hand.

"No trouble at all…didn't you say it yourself? Aren't I passing every day anyway, and I'd keep my social distance," the girl laughed while making an exaggerated backward step onto the road.

"Food…paint for that door, there…anything."

"Jobs get away from me."

"I'm sorry. I shouldn't be so pass-remarkable. We've only just met."

Now it was Eamon who laughed. "No offence taken. It's just I'm not as agile as I used to be," he said.

The girl stepped forward once more onto the footpath. "I could help you with that with your joints. I used to work in that line."

"If it doesn't kill me."

"Good…a few simple exercises every day. You will feel the benefit," the girl said as she made space for herself on the footpath, instructing Eamon to do likewise inside the gate.

"Just follow my lead," she said as she positioned herself.

"Feet nice and firm on the ground…legs together," she said as Eamon followed her lead.

"Arms outstretched and a nice little raise off your toes, five…four…three…two…one and relax," she instructed before repeating the exercise again while Eamon copied her movements awkwardly. The girl was warming to her task now.

"And when you have that mastered…legs together… up on the toes…right hand on right hip…left arm arced like so to the right over your head," she said, posing slowly to allow Eamon to complete the movement.

"Ah holy Jesus!" Eamon laughed as he lost his balance.

"Will you do those two for me four or five times a day for about five minutes a go?" she said as she stretched herself once more.

"I will," he answered.

"Promise."

"Yes Miss."

"You're welcome, and you can call me Sarah," she replied, starting to put her earphones back in.

"Pleased to meet you Sarah, and I'm Eamon," he said, giving her a playful army salute.

"Balance and posture, that's what it's all about, Eamon."

"I'll remember that."

"Good, and I've enjoyed our little chat," she continued.

"Sometimes it's nice to be nice. That's what I was brought up to believe," Eamon said.

"It's something I struggle with, to be honest," she answered wistfully. "Just enjoying a day for what it is. I overthink things Eamon and lately, I just…feel I've lost my way again."

"Everybody loses their way at some point in life," Eamon said quietly.

There was a brief silence before she spoke again.

"You see, I've…lost someone close."

"I'm very sorry to hear that."

"A while ago now, but it took a long time to come to terms with that and now these restrictions. It's a setback. Everything is so uncertain."

"Grief never leaves you. It just takes different forms, a sight, a sound, a smell, day of the week."

"Exactly and so today, Holy Thursday, that's our day now, and I know I shouldn't be up there, but I place a kiss on the headstone," she continued, her voice cracking with emotion.

"Loss never leaves you, Sarah."

"I'm sorry. I shouldn't be unburdening myself on you like this," she said, refocusing herself once more.

"You needn't apologise to me, girl. I've had loss too over the years, and loss needs to be shared sometimes…teased out…to make it bearable."

Sarah had stepped forward now and was resting a forearm across the pillar of Eamon's gate. They were within touching distance and Eamon could see a vulnerability in her eyes. He blinked the thought away.

"Do you believe Eamon?" she asked quietly.

"In what?"

"All of this," she said, drawing him in. "Life, heaven, hell…the whole shooting gallery."

"I used to."

Sarah laughed. "We have something in common, so."

"The Church shot itself in the foot and the people tarred everyone with the same brush," Eamon said as she stepped back once more and repositioned herself on the footpath.

"I pass two churches on my run every day now, locked up, silent and the world is still spinning on its axis. All those prayers unsaid, candles unlit and sins unforgiven," she said, gazing out into middle-distance.

"Did we ever think we would see the day," he said.

"Nobody saw this coming. The whole world brought to a standstill. A crash worse than 2008," she answered firmly.

"The best laid plans."

"I don't think I can face that again." There was a tiredness in her voice now.

"You're young, resilient."

"There's a real fear there now, Eamon."

"You will go and live your life when we come through this."

Sarah swept both of her hands back through her hair and arched her back.

"Did anyone ever tell you, you're easy to get on with," she said, facing skywards.

"People were always saying that at the school; "have a chat with Eamon, he's a good listener, he'll know what to do."

"You were a teacher."

"A brother," Eamon replied matter-of-factly.

"A brother," Sarah exclaimed, her eyes widening in surprise. "Aren't you the dark horse, and how long were you a brother?"

"I think I still am technically."

"My parents brought us to mass religiously every Sunday, but I just don't feel comfortable with that anymore."

"Do you mind if I ask why?"

"Because the world is unjust and full of pain. What type of God would create such a world?"

"I can't answer that for you…not anymore."

"You see it was my partner," Sarah continued, "the person I lost…Paul…in twenty twelve after the crash. Our business went under, something we had put our whole lives into, and he couldn't cope with that…handle it. Words can't describe when you lose someone like that to suicide."

Eamon took a breath before speaking: "I see."

"I'm sorry," Sarah said. "I shouldn't be doing this."

"What did I tell you about apologizing. Shur what else would I be doing? I enjoy the bit of company. The days can be long around here."

"And do you have any family yourself?" Sarah asked.

"A niece and a nephew, but they don't want much to do with me."

"I can't imagine."

"People make their own choices and there is a hurt in that".

There was a momentary silence before Eamon continued: "How did we end up going down that road!" he laughed.

"I know, as if we weren't depressed enough with lockdown as it is."

"At least you're smiling again," Eamon said.

"I am, aren't I," Sarah said as she began to put on her earphones again. "So…it was nice to meet you."

"I have a good one for you, before you go, if you have the time, that is."

"Of course."

Quickly, Eamon returned into the house and re-emerged holding a photograph. "Look at that," he said, stepping forward to place the photograph on the pillar before taking a step back. Sarah in turn stepped forward to the pillar and took the photograph in her hands. She scanned it; a black and white photograph of a schoolboy football team, a mix of smiling faces and closed eyes; one of the smaller boys in the centre awkwardly balancing a cup on his knees.

"Wow, the haircuts," she whistled.

"Nineteen seventy-four, School County champions," Eamon said as Sarah continued to scan the photograph.

"Gosh, there you are in the black," she said, indicating with her finger.

"I haven't changed that much, so," Eamon laughed.

"I'd know you out of it," she said, continuing to study the tall smiling figure at the rear of the photograph, a head of wavy black hair, flowing habit and clerical collar. Finally, after several moments, Sarah stepped forward and returned the photograph to the pillar.

"It must have been an interesting life, a nice memory to have."

"I was in South America the following year…Canada later on," Eamon said, once again taking the photograph in his hand as Sarah stepped back from the pillar. "Not as glamorous as it sounds, mind you. They liked to keep you humble, never liked you to get settled, over familiar," Eamon said, studying the photograph himself now.

"Would you believe two of those boys died young," Eamon said, "the goalkeeper," he continued, indicating with his finger to a tall good-looking boy with sallow blemish free skin and shoulder-length hair as both he and Sarah stepped closer to the pillar.

"Killed off a motorbike heading out to work one morning, and the small chap down the front there," Eamon said, now pointing out a small younger boy kneeling at the front of the photograph, hands on both knees, head tilted and a slightly quizzical look on a freckled face.

"That poor chap got himself into a spot of bother one night outside a bar…" Eamon's voice trailed off as he stepped away from the pillar once more.

"And do you have contact with any of the others now?" Sarah asked.

"About fifteen years ago, out of the blue."

"And what was that like?"

"It caught me unawares," he answered as Sarah took her phone from her pocket and stretched across the pillar, holding out the screen for Eamon to see.

"And here's a favourite of mine…with Paul."

Eamon looked at the photograph of the couple; Sarah, her auburn hair cut shorter in a neat bob, smiling directly at the camera, a circular pendant glistening in the sun, a green top accentuating a shapely figure. Paul in the foreground, fair hair, strong jawline and smiling broadly.

"He was a fine-looking chap," he said eventually.

"A stupid selfie," Sarah said, glancing at the photograph herself before returning the phone to her pocket. "That was the last photograph of the two of us together."

"And was there any indication…anything at all…any sign?"

"That I missed? To beat myself up?"

"No that's not. I didn't mean it like that."

"I really don't want to talk about it."

"Of course."

"I need to go."

"I'm sorry. I shouldn't have brought it up."

"You're fine. I just need to go, that's all."

"Please let me explain."

"Look, you're grand, but I'm just going to finish my run," she said, this time placing her earphones back in.

"Bye Eamon."

Eamon watched her as she jogged off into the distance, watched as she faded from view like a blue pixel. He paused and studied the old photograph again before returning inside.

Shit...you stupid bloody man!

Good Friday

Pit Pat...Pit Pat.

Sarah turned hesitantly at the wall and walked slowly on returning to the gate. The street was quiet. Wiping the sweat from her brow, she stood nervously before removing her backpack. Placing the bag on the pillar, she opened it and carefully removed a lily plant. Sarah then opened the gate, walked to the front door, set the plant down, knocked on the door softly before quickly returning to the street and closing the gate quietly behind her. As she re-clipped on her backpack, the front door opened tentatively.

"I brought you a gift, Eamon, for the day that's in it, to brighten up your garden if you want," she called out.

"You shouldn't have," Eamon said, opening the door fully. "You are very good," he added before bending down slowly to take up the plant and crossing to place it on the kitchen windowsill.

"And I have something small for you also," he said as he went back inside the house before returning with a postcard which he placed on the pillar, as Sarah took a step backwards.

"I wrote you a little note," he said, doing likewise, which allowed Sarah the opportunity to step forward and take the card.

"I got that from *An Post*…to send to someone."

"That's a lovely idea…thank you," Sarah said as she read the card.

"A peace offering for yesterday. I didn't mean to upset you like that. It was not my intention," Eamon said sheepishly.

"No. I was being…It was rude of me to bolt off like that. You were being nothing but kind to me."

"Friends again."

"Of course. It's very thoughtful of you," Sarah said as she skillfully unclipped her backpack in one movement and placed the card inside.

"Tell me more about the school, Eamon. It sounds fascinating," she said, readjusting her position on the footpath once more.

"There's nothing to tell. I went in every day and tried to do my best and let other people be the judge of me. You just wanted to make a difference. If I was to give you one piece of advice…I'd say you need to be bulletproof, no matter what life throws at you."

"We hadn't that…You see, we threw ourselves into the business…gyms…to such an extent it became an obsession, and it was so competitive trying to stay ahead, not just gyms, it was a concept. Paul drove it on, a whole lifestyle choice. One at first, then a second…a third in Boston…for the Irish, but it all came crashing down in two months. Everything we had worked for, built up, gone in a puff of smoke…the scale of it," Sarah said, wiping away a tear that was starting to form. "I miss him every day and now this…Would you believe that one virus in one country could bring the whole world to a standstill? Done in two days what the crash took two years to do."

"But maybe a good time to clear your head…step back and take stock. To view the world differently," Eamon answered.

"And stop running."

"Do you find benefit in it?" he asked.

"I dunno, to be honest. I suppose everybody is running from something in their own way. Anyway, the card is a nice gesture, Eamon," Sarah said, tapping her backpack. "That out of all the people, you chose me for one. It will go in pride of place on the mantelpiece."

"Good. I'm glad you like it."

"And the other one? Your niece or nephew?"

"God no."

"Why not?"

"There has been no contact for over ten years."

"And maybe this is as good a time as any to reach out."

"I embarrass them, but it is what it is, and your own family?"

"I have a sister in Sweden. We talk now more than ever, facetiming every other day. My parents…I miss the contact. They wouldn't be great with technology. They have always been there for me. My father. I think ye would get on. He is very…stoic. Paul didn't have that resilience."

"Different times," Eamon said, nodding.

"The press called us snowflakes."

"The press needs to label everybody."

"Mocked us…a whole generation not able to cope."

"I try not to listen to the news anymore."

"Especially now. It would overwhelm you. So, are you going to send the second card?" she asked.

"Maybe I'll give it to you, and you can write it!" Eamon said with a polite laugh.

"To who?"

"Yourself. Make a note of all those things you are not going to worry about anymore."

"There's a psychologist lost in you, Eamon!"

"We have to love ourselves sometimes if no one else will," Eamon said, stepping back to re-adjust the lily on the windowsill. "Thanks again for the plant."

"You're welcome, and have you been doing those exercises I showed you?"

"I am."

"Good…we'll take a look."

"You don't forget much."

"I'll lead you through it," Sarah said, standing with her feet together and arms outstretched. Eamon stepped forward and assumed the same starting position.

"Are you ready?" Sarah asked, holding her pose.

"I was just thinking," Eamon said, stifling a laugh.

"What? I could do with a giggle."

"The two of us."

"Go on."

"Standing like this on a Good Friday. Which one of us is the Good Thief?"

Easter Saturday

Night

It was the reflection of the light that caught Eamon's eye, a shimmering mirage dancing in the street, erratically at first and then with a rhythm that drew him almost hypnotically to his kitchen window. He drew the curtain back and there in the half-light he could see the familiar figure of Sarah standing by the pillar where a lantern was now placed. He watched for a moment, and she appeared transfixed, the glow from the lantern bestowing on her an ethereal beauty. Eventually, he moved from the window, opened his door and stepped into the garden.

"This is a nice surprise," he said in greeting.

"The whole country is shining a light for the frontline workers, and I wanted to share that with a friend."

"And I am delighted to see you. I missed you this morning."

"I took a break," she said, the light flickering across her face. "So, I'm here now instead."

"And an unexpected pleasure it is. The evenings can be long."

"In fact, my doctor has told me to scale back on the running."

"Nothing serious, I hope."

"Not at all, a change of lifestyle, that's all."

"Good. I will get two chairs," Eamon said, and he went back into the house before returning, placing one chair at the front door and passing the second one out over the gate to Sarah.

"I was stopped on my way over here, another check-point. The city is in a grip," she said, sitting down.

"And what did you say?" Eamon said, pausing at the gate.

"They turned me back; said I was flouting the rules."

"But you still made it," he said, also sitting down.

"Where there's a will!"

"You must be public enemy number one at this stage," Eamon said as the crackle of distant fireworks suddenly rumbled across the sky.

"Ah, that's a nice touch. You can make them out in the distance there," Sarah said, standing up to scan the horizon. Eamon also stood and approached the pillar to join her. Sarah took a step nearer to the road and they both stood in silence for several minutes until the sounds finally faded, and the colours merged into the night sky. Neither of them spoke and Sarah coughed quietly to clear her throat:

"Darkness coming down."
In another part of town
Between two spires
A slogan written down.
Is there much more to life?

The sweetness of her voice cut through the night air:

"Remember Cain and Abel"
Brothers from the start

The hate that came between them

Tears us apart.

Eamon watched her closely as she continued in note-perfect harmony:

"Darkness coming down."

In another part of town

Singer on the corner

Sings

"Watch the moon come down."

And then silence again. Somewhere, a dog barked, and an engine turned.

"My…that's very beautiful," Eamon said quietly.

"Paul wrote it."

"And you sing it perfectly."

"He had wanted to do something in music, but he let it go."

"It's a beautiful gift to remember him by."

"And now you," Sarah said firmly.

"Pardon?"

"A song for the frontline workers."

"Me? I don't sing."

"You must have some party-piece," she insisted.

"No, seriously, not a note."

"Come on!"

"God's truth. Would I lie to you at this stage?"

Sarah laughed: "I dunno…would you?"

"Absolutely not, and you after risking incarceration to be here in the first place!"

They both sat again.

"Well, it's an Easter I never thought I would see," Eamon said.

"The new normal, Eamon."

"And have you a plan yourself to get back on track?"

"Workwise, I will be slowing down for a while. That's for sure."

"That sounds positive."

"I needed to re-evaluate, and I did."

"Good for you."

In the distance, the only sounds to be heard now were of the city re-adjusting to the new normal; the aberration of the crackling fireworks fading from memory as both Eamon and Sarah sat in their respective *bubbles* and chatted late into the night by the glow of a fading lantern.

Easter Sunday

Eamon hadn't slept well. It had been a late finish, and he had warned her about crossing the city at that late hour.

"Young girls took massive risks," he thought to himself. *"They don't see bad in people."*

Every day, the news was full of horror stories. Young girls taking risks. He parted the net curtain. The chairs where they had sat on them.

"Too trusting for her own good."

She was dressed smartly and casually this Easter morning; a *Centra* bag incongruous in her left hand.

"You made it home alright."

"No problem at all. There were people out across the city in their gardens chatting. There was a great sense of unity there. Everybody in good form like no other Saturday I remember."

"Once you were safe."

"I told you I'd be fine," she said, stepping forward to the pillar. "Happy Easter…I brought you a gift…something small," she said, taking a small tin of paint and some brushes from the bag and placing them on the pillar. "I had these in the shed. A job I never got round to." She stepped back from the pillar.

"You shouldn't have," Eamon said, taking his cue to step forward and take the paint and brushes.

"I thought it might be nice, to freshen up the door there, something to do."

"Many happy returns," Eamon said, taking up the items and setting them down at the front door.

"I brought us breakfast as well," Sarah continued, taking a roll and a bottle of water from the bag and placing them also on the pillar. "I went for ham and cheese. Is that ok?"

"Perfect."

"And butter."

"Has to be butter," Eamon agreed, taking the food and water.

"I threw in some extra water," Sarah said, removing her own roll and a bottle of water before placing the bag on the pillar. "To keep you hydrated for the painting."

"Yes, boss," Eamon answered, taking the bag and placing it carefully beside the paint and brushes. They both sat and began to eat in silence.

"Can I ask you something, Eamon?" Sarah asked before taking a drink of her water.

"Fire away."

"And you can tell me to bog off if you want, but do you miss it, the religious life?"

"I suppose I do. The day to day, helping others, but I want to be honest with you."

"In what way?"

"You see there was an investigation."

"What kind of investigation?"

"Into the football team in nineteen seventy-four. They said I singled out one of the boys for special attention."

"And did you?"

"A throwaway comment about his new boots. Adidas with the white soles."

"And what happened?" Sarah asked, placing what remained of her roll on her lap. Eamon took a sip from his drink before answering.

"Nothing came of it. I was a role model for God's sake, someone to look up to."

"And that was the end of it?"

"They just wouldn't leave it alone. They kept digging, and I had visited the boy once, Brian, in the sick bay."

"Eamon, did anything happen?" Sarah asked firmly.

"They tried to twist it…said he wasn't himself after that. They felt he had become uncomfortable…teary. Of course, he was. The boy was alone, sick, away from home."

"And did you explain all that, your side of the story?"

"That was the end of it. Nothing was ever proven."

"And what did they accuse you of?"

"Inappropriate behaviour," Eamon said without a hint of emotion, before settling back into his chair and going on to outline to Sarah how he might have given the boy "a little hug", that it was almost fifty years ago, so difficult to remember the exact detail, that the boy had made nothing of it, but how Eamon had never set foot in that school again. Occasionally, as he spoke, he stopped to take some food and sip a drink while Sarah listened intently and examined the pain on his face as he described how "they wouldn't let it rest", how nobody had said anything directly, but the innuendo had stuck. His family had lost trust in him, and eventually, they started to move him about, South America to start with and then Canada to clear the air:

"To take a programme, therapy, a clinic, a sex clinic, as if what I had done was low, sordid."

"And you agreed."

"I had blind faith. Not to go would have been an admission of guilt."

An uncomfortable silence descended between them, Sarah finishing her food and drinking liberally.

"Well?" Eamon finally asked, piercing the silence, but Sarah appeared oblivious and folded her food wrapping neatly.

"Say something," he continued.

"I don't know what to say," Sarah said after a thought.

"Have I stunned you? I just wanted to be straight and honest with you."

"I appreciate that."

"That was a loss for me...my way of life."

"Of course. And what became of the boy after?"

"I never saw him again, but the seed was sown and then contact was made, out of the blue in two thousand and five. This boy...man was looking to press charges."

"Jesus, what did you do?" Sarah said, sitting forward.

"Fight it, of course, to protect my good name. It was a bloody nightmare."

"What happened?"

"Nothing. Again, but the process nearly broke me mentally. This man, he saw an opportunity, and they basically put me under house arrest. Lockdown before lockdown was invented."

"It must have been a traumatic experience for you."

"Five years with that hanging over me."

"And did you at least get an apology?"

"No…nothing."

"You must have been delighted, though. I can only imagine the sense of release."

"It was bittersweet. You see, when his legal team finally traced the other boys for corroborating statements...the two supposed witnesses had passed away."

"Those boys from the photograph," Sarah emitted a low whistle.

"Yes...it left it all up in the air, inconclusive, and the sword of Damocles hanging over my head."

Silence gripped them both again.

"And did you Eamon, from one friend to another, have a moment of weakness? I'm sorry, I have to ask," Sarah said calmly."

"No, and it's I should be apologising to you. I just want everything out in the open. No secrets. I'm done with that," Eamon answered, his voice sounding tired.

"I appreciate you being so candid with me," Sarah said as Eamon stood up slowly and approached the pillar. He looked older to her now more than anytime over the last three days, and he stood at the gate as if his plinth and continued in a measured tone:

"And when it all died down, they allowed me to drift. Shortly after I moved in here, the local press wanted to do a story on me: "in the council house at someone else's expense". I wouldn't engage with them, so they went ahead and did the story anyway, got their pound of flesh in the public interest. That finished me with the neighbours."

"And your niece and nephew."

"Yes."

Once more, the silence reasserted itself.

"What are you thinking?" Eamon asked. He seemed relaxed once more.

"I tend to make my own mind up about people."

"And have you changed your opinion of me?"

"I think I am a good judge of character," Sarah said, standing up energetically. "Well, that's me done Eamon. I've got to fly." She handed the chair back over the gate to Eamon in one movement, and then placed her neatly folded wrapping paper and empty water bottle on the pillar.

"Right, I'll be off then," she said before preparing to leave.

"Sarah," Eamon called after her as she set off down the footpath.

"Yes," she answered, turning briefly to face him once more.

"You believe me don't you about the boys?"

"Does it matter?" she replied, turning again to continue her journey.

"It matters to me," Eamon said softly, but she was gone. He watched her depart into the distance before finally turning to face his faded front door. He glanced at the paint and brushes. At least he had a job to do. That would keep him occupied.

Bank Holiday Monday

"They say painting is therapeutic," Eamon thought to himself. *"Brings an organisation and discipline to the thought process."* Eamon was lost in concentration, carefully navigating the door handle with the fine edge of the brush.

Pit pat…Pit pat

"Morning Eamon. You are up at it early," Sarah called out, stopping at the gate and removing her earphones.

"You were spot on," Eamon answered, glancing quickly over his shoulder in her direction without breaking his brush stroke rhythm. "This place does need a bit of a makeover."

"You won't know yourself," Sarah said as Eamon stood up slowly, stepped back from the work and set down the paint brush carefully.

"You came," he said, turning to face Sarah directly. "I wasn't expecting you this morning."

"And why not?"

"Weren't you saying you had to take a break from running for a while."

"I do...and is that the only reason that you weren't expecting me?"

"I suppose it wasn't," Eamon said hesitantly. "To be honest, people tend to steer clear of me when they get wind of my story."

"I didn't get wind of it," Sarah shrugged.

"No, that's true. You got it from the horses' mouth."

"One of the horses," she shot back quickly.

"Touché."

"Anyways I have a couple of confessions of my own to make," Sarah said as she leaned across the gate. "When I got home yesterday, my curiosity got the better of me."

"That killed the cat, you know."

"I googled you. Your story."

"And is it there in all its glory?"

"Nothing is private anymore...a couple of clicks."

"And did you find anything incriminating?"

"The newspaper article."

"And your verdict?"

"A lot of smoke and mirrors, to be fair."

"That passes for news now," Eamon said tiredly.

Sarah stood back from the gate once more and took a breath: "It's just...I felt a sense of guilt after I did that. That I didn't take what you confided in me at face value."

"It is what it is," Eamon answered.

"Are you upset…that I went hunting?"

"You have been nothing but kind to me, and the second confession?"

"I'm not going to be around for a while...doctor's orders."

"Nothing serious, I hope."

"No nothing like that. It's just I'm fourteen weeks pregnant."

"I'm pleased for you."

"I went down the donor route...I.V.F. It's not something I pursued lightly. I thought long and hard about bringing my life down a different road and now since lockdown the doubts have come flooding back. A snowflake baby for a snowflake child, but and I know we only met since Thursday, I think you have shown me, given me a new belief and opened my eyes to the bigger picture," Sarah spoke measuredly until her voice trailed off into the still morning air.

"Will I see you again?"

"You will."

"I'd like that."

"And now you can do me one favour?" Sarah said, composing herself once more.

"If I can."

"Can I have that second postcard if you don't mind?"

"Of course."

"And another look at that photograph from nineteen seventy-four?"

"To satisfy your curiosity?"

"To help you, like you have helped me. Will you allow me to do that?"

"I will," Eamon said, going back into the house and returning to place both items on the pillar. Sarah stepped forward and took a pen from her backpack:

"As I'm not going to be around as much, I'd like to write a note for you," she said, beginning to write. "To remember me by," she added before stepping back once more and allowing Eamon to step forward.

"Keep that somewhere safe, Eamon."

"That's a lovely sentiment," Eamon said, reading the card slowly. "I will treasure it."

"I thought it was appropriate."

"Very, and the photograph," Eamon asked as he put the card in his pocket.

"These boys Eamon. I think you need to let them go," Sarah said, stepping up to the pillar and taking the photograph in her hand. "There's nothing to be gained by looking backwards, and I could help you with that," she said, taking a lighter from her backpack and lighting it. "What do you say?"

"Memories," Eamon said quietly.

"Not all good. Just say the word."

"If you think it would help," Eamon continued as Sarah took her cue and lit the photograph and rested it back down on the pillar. They both watched in silence as the photograph curled and quickly reduced to melted ash.

"May all the bad luck go with it," Sarah said as the last ringlets of smoke disappeared.

"New beginnings."

"And I was thinking...if it's a boy, to name the child...Paul…Paul…Eamon. How do you feel about that?"

"I'm lost for words to be truthful…I'm moved...thank you."

"And thanks to you I'm not scared anymore," Sarah said, her voice brimming with emotion.

"Come here girl. Let me give you a hug," Eamon said, stepping towards the gate and Sarah also stepped forward to open the latch on the gate.

"I shouldn't," she said, composing herself before stopping to close the gate again. "But you know what I can do Eamon, a photograph of the two of us, a bank holiday selfie!" Quickly she took out her phone and quickly set up the shot, both on either side of the gate.

"Hold it there now Eamon…three...two…one...done," Sarah said triumphantly before showing Eamon the photograph.

"That's not too bad at all," she laughed.

"An end to a great weekend."

"It was good," she agreed, placing her phone back in her backpack.

"Like no other."

"The new normal."

They both stood and breathed in a comfortable reflective silence.

"The place has never looked better," Eamon said, turning to face the house.

"A lick of paint does wonders."

"I will finish that off there now. It will keep me going for the day."

"Right. I won't keep you any longer, so," Sarah said, and she untangled her earphones. "And thanks again for everything… I was pleased to get to know you."

"Likewise."

"I'll be off so," Sarah said, turning to take her leave.

"Sarah"

"Yes," she answered, glancing back at Eamon.

"You are going to be ok."

"And so are you," Sarah called out brightly, as her auburn hair glistened in the early morning sun.

Pit pat... Pit pat...

The Blue Line

Grace had explained to them both that the train would be a forty-minute ride to the airport and that it would take them through to the main terminal. She had also thanked her sister-in-law Clare and niece Samantha for coming; "for making the effort", as they exchanged the platitudes that people engaged in at funerals before hugging briefly and parting ways. "It was the least we could do," Clare had said offhandedly, before adding it was what her late brother David "would have wanted."

Her daughter Samantha had been a somewhat reluctant attendee, complaining frequently in the run-up to the trip that it was just "too much hassle, that amount of travel for two days" for an uncle she didn't even know, but her mother was adamant. They were representing the family and David had been very good to them both when her own husband, Samantha's father, had passed, but Samantha had been too young to remember that.

The train hummed away from the platform and as both women settled into their seats, Clare thought of David one more time. She had done a lot of that over the previous forty-eight hours. She remembered how it was in her, he had confided his love for this bohemian American girl, and she thought of those long conversations where he had spoken of not "planning it to happen" and asking for advice on how he might smooth things over with their mother as the relationship was about to bring his burgeoning studies for the priesthood to a shuddering halt.

Clare pressed her cheek to the cold windowpane to get some respite from the stifling heat. She smiled to herself. Their mother *had* blown a gasket. The bishop was brought in, but even he couldn't stop the young lovers. Mother blamed Grace for everything, for "ruining the family". She never forgave her for it. The wedding was a low-key affair, but mother retracted her threats of non-attendance to sit in all her finery because; "she wouldn't let it be said" as she put it herself. Clare looked across at her daughter seated opposite her, diligently scrolling her iPhone. This was her time now, and Clare looked forward to watching her take her place in the world. That was *her* life now, a spectator of other people's milestones.

At stops, Clare watched the commuters embark and disembark, business-like, determined people who had also made lives like David had done. Perhaps he too had made this same daily journey in his prime, but she couldn't be sure, as regular contact had been lost over the years from either side of the Atlantic. She looked at her daughter again, detached from the hustle and bustle of the daily commute. The college fees had put Clare to the pin of her collar, but she was determined that Samantha would remain driven. "Take a chill pill

Mam…you're on holiday," was Samantha's response when Clare had tried to broach the subject on the flight over. Clare had reprimanded her daughter then about it being " a strange holiday" they were on, and Grace had indeed given an open invitation that they were both welcome back at any time under better circumstances.

People said all sorts of things at funerals.

David's last visit home was the perfect case in point, their own mother's funeral. He had travelled alone, and she remembered how, standing in the backyard, he had told Clare that Grace found such big family events difficult and "all that went with them." He had also spoken about how they were both very happy forging their new life together in Boston and how every single day was full of surprises; "unexpected, pleasant interludes with people who enrich my life." For her part, Clare felt he sounded tired that night and that some of the fire had dimmed. He appeared happy to have companionship, "someone to talk to in the evening," as he put it, but she had admired his resolve not to let life scar him.

Clare allowed herself to drift. She too had to re-calibrate after the death of her husband. Her friends told her to "get back out there" and there had been an opportunity once, a teacher at Samantha's primary school. She had spoken to him a few times in the yard, and he had made a phone call once about a school matter, but she didn't encourage him. It had been nice, the attention, the thought that someone might think of her in that way, but she couldn't do it. She had loved her husband too much.

She took out her own mobile now. When she had last spoken to David on the phone, he had been a very sick man. He had it all arranged and made it seem quite natural and reassuring. He spoke about being positive and reconciled with the diagnosis. "We live and die and that's the end of it," he had said quietly. At the time, she hadn't known what to say, particularly when he spoke about having "disappointed" his mother and having ultimately lived "an average life with an average result."

Clare scrolled through the photographs Samantha had taken of herself and Grace that morning as they left the house. Clare hadn't known what to expect on this trip and had secretly hoped that David might be buried in Ireland. The crematorium had been tough for her, but not as impersonal as she had feared. Grace was smiling weakly in the photographs, and deep-down Clare knew they would never meet again.

Opposite her, Samantha remained lost in her music. She was the future now, and as Clare put the phone away, she surrendered herself to thoughts of the night her own Denis passed. She remembered the strange feeling of him going cold as she held him, but also of being fully aware that this was a precious, beautiful moment as special as anything they had ever shared in their short time together. Seeing him take his last breath was what their life had come down to, but in that instant, she knew everything had been worth it, and she wouldn't have changed an inch of it. She caught her reflection in the train carriage window, and a tear rolled involuntarily down her cheek.

"Mam?"

"Yes, love," Clare answered as the train glided to a halt.

"I'm glad I came."

"Good…and so am I."

Winged

Cork Prison

Bluerock
Crown rock
Snowy
Blue checker
Squealer
Poulter
Tumbler
Fantail
Antwerp
Reds
Greys
Pink-Necked
Bleeding-Heart

I like pigeons.
They don't hurt me.
Pigeons come back.
When I was twelve, my pigeon won a race.
Me dad is a sausage.

Me mam loves darts.
Christy said, "Don't worry, I'll be back."

I told him I was alright.
Told him I was with Murphy and Ring.
Told me the pigeons were fine.
Told me Luigi got stabbed outside *Zicos.*
Told me Taz Daly did it.
They were drinking all day together.
Christy said he wouldn't sort it.
Told me he is fed up with all that shit, Luigi would have to sort it himself when he got out of the CUH.
Lucky to be alive, he said.
Bleeding all over the place he was.
Some *bure* passing saved him.
Put her fingers in his neck to stop the bleeding, she did.
Asked Christy how was mam?
"You know mam," he says.
Told him I don't want help from no screws.

The Governor is a proper spud, and the screws are all pricks. I told the judge I'd do two years on my back... two years for a scabby car and some houses. Did them coz I wanted to. I needed some money, so I robbed the houses, and I needed the car to get away from the houses. Christy ran this place when he was inside. No one messed with him.

Told me to keep the head down.
Reckons I'll do 18 months.

18 months with Murphy and Ring.
Another couple of spuds.

All the screws are sausages...pure langers.
Ring another sausage.
Said he'd knock my block off.
He would yeah.
Christy would dig him around the place.

Me mam and dad came yesterday.
Me mam annoying me about keeping myself clean.
Me dad shouting.
Calling me a waster.

A fool.

Me dad calling me a disgrace to the family.

Me mam saying, "don't listen to him, boy."

Telling me Christy couldn't come.

He has a job labouring at The Events Centre now.

Me dad shouting, telling me Christy has no time to be minding shagging birds.

Saying he has a good mind to "fuck that loft off the roof."

Me mam telling me Christy goes up to the loft all the time.

Telling me someone broke up Taz Daly's loft.

She read it on Facebook.

Me dad shouting: "I'm no son of his…a fucking mistake."

A mistake.
Me dad.
That's what he thinks.
His own son.
A mistake.
I'll do two years on me back.
He's a fucking wanker.
I'd kill him.
I don't want no more visits.
They're fucking stupid!
They don't know what I want.
I want to go…
To sleep.
To find a dream.
My dream.
About an angel.
A good one in heaven.
She held my hand, and we went for a walk outside.
All over heaven we walked.
Looking for God.
But we couldn't find him anywhere.
I wanted to see him…find him coz I think he is sad.
Coz, we met lots of people walking in the dream.
Sad people.
Just walking…walking around…not smiling.
Not laughing.
Blank.
And I want to be like them.

Miss Cotter wants me to read and write.

Wants me to read a book.
Says I can't just sit and look at the cell wall all day.
Told her I can't do no writing.
Told her it's gammy.
Wants me to learn.
Told her my last teacher was a fucking spud.
Hated him.
Wants me to read.
Told me Christy and Luigi were good lads.
Did their exams here.
Said Christy was a great worker.
Did his Junior Cert and wrote letters home.
Wants me to write.
Can't write.
Wants to show me.
Told her I like horses.
Robbed the Stokes' ones up The Tank Field.
Told her I keep pigeons out my back.

She smells nice.

Christy said he'd give her one.
Miss Cotter.
Not a bother, he said.
Even though she has a kid herself.
They all would.
Murphy and Ring.
Christy would dig Ring around the place.
Told me if he ever laid a finger on me… a fucking finger…
Told me he would do him.

And Murphy too. And Christy said Luigi just walked out.

Took all the shit off his arms and got the bus home.

Rang Christy straight away, asking would he get him a shooter.

That he wanted to kill someone.

Show them who's boss.

Christy making me swear to say nothing to Murphy or Ring.

Says Murphy is a rat to the screws.

Told me he wouldn't fix it for Luigi.

Told me he is keeping his head down…nose clean.

Wants me to do the same.

Do the time and fuck the rest of them.

A bunch of sausages.

Christy says if Ring even looks at me funny…even once.

Ring.

Always messing with your head.

Every day.

Morning.

Evening.

Night.

Wrecking your head.

"Only messing," Ring says.

"Only messing, Danny boy."

I miss my birds.

I miss my mam.

Christy!!!

Miss Cotter wants me to learn to read and write properly.

When I get out, she says there are plenty of places… good places.

She wants to help.

Told her I'd do another six months on me back.

Told her I'd pull the cell down.

Told her to fuck off.

Told her I want to go.

Don't want to do no fucking reading and writing.

Told her I want to go.

Want to lie down.

To sleep.

Find my dream.

Told her to fuck off.

It's my dream.

Met Luigi there.

In my dream.

Told me he was going to sort the dirty piss bed Daly's.

That they may never have an hours' luck for every day on this earth.

That on his soul he'll have them all murdered.

Stop Luigi!

Christy tried to help you. He tried to fucking help you!!

Miss Cotter.

"ABCDEFG…nothing hurts Daniel like me."

Miss Cotter won't help me.
Christy shanked good and proper.
Some bure passing.
Christy dying.
Christy bleeding all over the place.
Ring laughing.
Miss Cotter wants me to write for her.
Christy messing with my head.
Me dad.
"Christy has a job now. Hasn't time for fuckology."
Stay away from me dad!
Me dad telling me I have some nerve expecting him to be minding those birds and cleaning their shit.
Feeding.
Cleaning.
Telling me he will stuff their faces until they burst.
Feathers everywhere.
Ring unbuttoning my shirt.
Telling me don't say a word, Daniel love.
Kissing me.
Making a man of me.
Ring stop!!
Wants me inside him.
No Ring.
Stop.
Dad.
Stop!!
Luigi.
Stop!!!
Miss Cotter!!!

The screws think I'm stupid.
Me mam doesn't get me.
Told me I was getting involved in a bad game.
Told them I feel fine.
Told her I feel sad and happy.
Told them I wouldn't eat.
Not to be annoying me.
Screws are rats.
They should get a fucking life.
Told them to fuck off.

I'm just not well.
Tell me mam.
I've done nothing wrong.
I'm sorry.
I didn't mean it.
Me mam doesn't understand.
The voices.
I want to go somewhere better.
With the angel.
I would like that.
Somewhere I can explain.
How I feel.
That I don't want to live.
Blah Blah Blah.

About the Author

If you feel generous and have a couple of minutes, please leave a review where you purchased this book. It makes a huge difference to the author. Thank you in advance.

Derek O'Gorman a teacher by profession is an award winning playwright and published author based in Cork City, Ireland. Among his awards are The VSA Playwright Award, The Cork Arts Theatre Playwright Award, UCC DRAMAT Playwright Award, and the UCC Alumni Short Story Award. His work has won the All-Ireland One-Act play award on two occasions, been produced on RTE National Radio, and been adapted for short films (most notably for the Cork Midsummer Festival in 2021). Derek is also a football coach at UCC AFC. He lives in Cork City wih his wife Deirdre.

Follow the author on X at @OgormanDerek.

About the Publisher

Sulis International Press publishes select fiction and nonfiction in a variety of genres under four imprints: Riversong Books, Sulis Academic Press, Sulis Press, and Keledei Publications.

For more, visit the website at
https://sulisinternational.com

Subscribe to the newsletter at
https://sulisinternational.com/subscribe/

Follow on social media
https://www.facebook.com/SulisInternational
https://x.com/Sulis_Intl
https://www.pinterest.com/Sulis_Intl/
https://www.instagram.com/sulis_international/

Milton Keynes UK
Ingram Content Group UK Ltd.
UKHW010724130923
428592UK00001B/8